THE
REVENGE
OF THE
STONED
RATS

"The novel revolves around the likeable character of teenage wimp Billy Sikes whose vision of modern Ireland is coloured by his dysfunctional adoptive family, his legendary half-brother Herbert and a cast of friends and foes who slip in and out of allegory, not to mention life and death, with the ease of champion figure skaters. Psychedelia grounded in street dialogue is at least as good a tag as surrealism: Billy lives in a waking nightmare much of the time, but the reader gets an ongoing chance to feel clever at allusion-spotting, as Holy and Unholy trinity swap sides with alarming frequency. There are several contenders for the role of The Prince himself. Wholly herself, however, is Billy's hefty and horrible cousin Agnes, sociopath par excellence: the sort of girl who would pull the legs of horses, cackling the while and a truly remarkable comic creation."

Sharon Barnes, In Dublin *magazine*

THE REVENGE

OF THE

STONED
RATS

The novel previously known as The Prince

EDDIE SMYTH

 PUBLICATIONS

This edition first published 2018
Published in Ireland
A **JRi** Publication

The moral right of the author has been asserted in accordance
with the Copyright And Related Rights Act, 2000.

Print ISBN: 978-1-5272-2605-0

This is a work of fiction. Any resemblance to any persons,
living or dead, is entirely coincidental.

Design by www.carrowmore.ie

Printed by TJ International Ltd, Padstow, Cornwall

Eddie Smyth was born in Dublin in 1961. He has worked as a stores and warehouse operative, forklift driver, motorcycle courier, and as a door-to-door and telephone salesperson. His novel, *The Prince,* was published in 1996.

INTRODUCTION

What are you fuckin' lookin' at? Well ... ? I've a pain in me bollocks with all this. So you read introductions, do you! What are you some kind of academic or college kid? Were you told to read this? Is it proscribed reading? What fuckin' professor, or whatever up-his-own-arse dickhead teaches you, would proscribe this shit? Or, maybe you're just the kind of wanker who doesn't just skip to the story, like everyone else.

He couldn't just leave well enough alone, the skinny little bastard! He reckons that "The Prince" was never finished, but it's the same fuckin' story, and it's still a pack of lies! So if you haven't paid for it yet, don't be wastin' your bleedin' time or your money, that's unless you get a loan of it from your mate, or, if you are a regular sham, you stroke it from Eason's, same as I fuckin' did with the last one!

Go back to your iPod, or your Playstation or whatever shite youse are all into these days. You won't know what he's on about anyway, you and your fuckin' college degree! What would you know about the 1970s? Bet you never even heard of Pipi Longstocking, or Voyage to the Bottom of the Sea, or Mart and Market, or Elric of Melnibone, or Johnny Forty Coats, or even Puff the Magic bleedin' Dragon! Whatever about skinhead gangs, or skullin' flagons in the fields, or gettin' the bit of tit of a young wan, or being dragged to mass and teachers batin' ye, and all that other shite that he craps on about. And don't bleedin' start me about the war in the North!

Oh yeah, It's still full of big words, but you'll like that, won't you! Maybe you're some kind of intellectual, same as the skinny, bad-mouthing bollocks must think he is; he must have had a dictionary shoved up his arse! Well I'm telling you now, when I get the little bastard he'll be pickin' one out of his teeth!

He thinks he's so fuckin' smart, but the lying, deranged, little toe-rag still hasn't got a pot to piss in. And I'm no gombeen; how do you think I got the fuckin' Jag! I'm smarter than he'll ever be, and I'm not going away either, he'll find out.

The Black Prince, 2018

PROLOGUE

Jesus Christ died on the cross, so did he: my brother Herbert. My brother Herbert died on "The Cross": a junction in Dublin, near where we lived. He was also set upon by unbelievers, doubters and worshippers of false gods who, in his case, bludgeoned him to death with bald heads, bars, stones and Doc Martin boots. But he too would rise again. So I waited until he did.

Just a matter of time, that's what I'd said to myself: "It's just a matter of time." But I didn't like matters of time, because when time matters, it messes around with you: it doesn't do what you want it to do, you don't try to make it go fast or slow; you just sit back and wait - let it happen – and it did!

I wasn't worried about what way he'd announce himself, but I knew that he wouldn't just walk up to me on the street, and say something like, "Hello Billy, long time no see!" That wasn't his way; he had much more subtle, meaningful, approaches to all things. So,when he did reappear, I could smile, and say to myself, "Death hasn't changed you."

It was when I was skipping my way home through some wasteland, to avoid the drudges that I had to work with, that he appeared from behind an ancient tree, one of a small group of survivors along the way, and having taking on the appearance of an old, hunched-over, grey-haired man wearing a worn-out overcoat (he was actually tall and dark!), he, proffering the remains of a cigarette, said: "Give us a light there son!"

I felt like laughing, and saying to him: "You're the 'Son,' and our father has enough light for both of us," but, instead, I played along with him, although probably with a bit of a smirk on my face, and dipped into my pocket for my matches. Now, I must have only taken my eyes of him a second, but when I arose, he was gone. He could have slipped back into the trees again, but I knew better than to look.

He was gone, but he was back!

PART 1

1973

Now that he was back, if was going to be like it was before, I wouldn't mind. Before, often didn't seem that bad when you thought about it afterwards. "We'll laugh about this in years to come," they used to say (Was it in a book or a film?). I never stopped laughing! He taught me how to do that. He taught me almost everything.

I say "almost" because he didn't try to teach me anything that wasn't that important. I lived with my Aunt Kate, and she did that. Aunt Kate and school, although school wasn't as good at it. She taught me how to read and count. I needn't have gone to school at all: It didn't teach me anything! Secondary school was worse to me than primary school; I couldn't see any point in it. In primary school, I suppose, I didn't think like that, because in primary school I hadn't, for the most of it, known him yet. I didn't stay too long in secondary school.

In primary school, my mother's name was Jezebel, at least for a while. I told people and they thought that it was funny, because they were only about six or eight too, and Jezebel Sikes was a funny name where we came from.

My Aunt Kate wasn't amused, though, when I said it to her, which I didn't think fair, because it was from her that I'd heard if first. I understand that she hadn't actually said it to me, but I'd heard her say it to another Aunt, whom everyone said they couldn't stand, at least, when she wasn't there. But when Kate finished shouting, she told me that my mother's name was actually Maureen – I preferred Jezebel!

She didn't tell me much else about my mother, but I overheard plenty more conversations about her e.g: She went across to England and had a baby when the war was on. The baby's name was Herbert, and the war stopped. As my mother said she didn't understand where the baby came from, she'd insisted that she must have been 'immaculately concepted.' We'd been told about that in school, but I hadn't a clue what it meant. But it was a good story, and it was religion, so it had to be true!

But it seemed that no one believed my mother, and when I asked Aunt Kate about it, she shouted at me again, and gave me what she called a "clip on the ear," which was, in reality, a slap across the head, and warned me not be thinking about things that I couldn't understand. But, even so, I was to tell the priest all about it, the next time that I was sent to confession.

Word had it then, that Herbert and my mother went to live with an Aunt of hers, that my Aunt Bridgit, that's the one that no one liked, claimed that she, herself, couldn't abide, and stayed there until my own father came along, who was, apparently, 'a dangerous man'.

Because he was a dangerous man, I supposed, my mother couldn't chance taking Herbert with her when she took off with him to; a flat in London; the South of France; a caravan in Lancashire; a bedsit in Birmingham; a travelling circus (I was never convinced about that one; I think Brigit was on the drink that day!), then back to Ireland, where they got married before I was born, so that my mother wouldn't have another "little bastard."

They called me William because, with Sikes, my father thought that it was funny, or clever, or something. It was later in my life before I knew why.

My father died, and it seems, "peacefully in his bed." Which the "likes of him" didn't deserve, my Aunt Bridgit said.

"Jezebel" took off again then, and landed me with Aunt Kate.

Maybe living in Kate's wasn't so bad because I didn't know of anything better, or maybe it was good because I knew no worse, I doubt if I really thought about it: it just was! Anna was too, and so was Agnes – especially!

Anna and Agnes were Kate's daughters. Their father was dead. That was about the only thing, it seemed, he had in common with mine: He didn't smoke or drink; he didn't gamble; he'd great respect for his wife and for his children; he went to work everyday and gave Kate all his money, and then, when he was still only thirty-five, he died, because, as Kate said: "God takes the good when they're young." My father wasn't young: he was far too old, allegedly, even for my mother.

Agnes would live for ever – she was an ogre! She was about a year younger than Anna, and one year older than me, but she was a lot wider, rounder and thicker than either of us. She loved to grab me by the hair, and pinch my arms, and then, maybe, drag me with her "friends" (they weren't really, they just pretended to be because of their fear!) up to the pond at the back of us and duck me into it, to send me home wet and filthy, so that Kate wouldn't let me out again for days. She did lots of other things as well.

She couldn't bother Anna. Kate said that Anna was "for the birds." Anna sat and looked at the walls with a smile on her face. Even if she sat in front of the television, you could come into the room, and say: "What's on Anna?" and she'd say: "I haven't a clue!" She wouldn't try and bluff her way out of it, or pretend that she didn't hear the question, she'd just say: "I haven't a clue!" She was honest, was Anna.

If, and I say "if" because you'd hardly be foolish enough if you knew her, although I have to admit that I was once or twice, and she could tell you if she wanted to because she 'followed' things, you asked Agnes the same question, she'd much more than likely say: "Will you shut the fuck up, I'm watching this!" or, "Get the fuck out out of the room and close the bleedin' door behind you, you stupid little bastard!"

She called me "a bastard," or, "the bastard," when she wasn't talking at me, all the time, even though I knew that I wasn't. Like I said, I'd overheard the conversations.

Anna did other things apart from looking at nothing. She cooked and she cleaned (Agnes was a slob.), because Kate had a job and couldn't be at home, as she often told us: "Twenty-four hours a day." She read and played chess, mostly on her own. I say "mostly" because she showed me how to play and we had the occasional game. The occasional swift game, because her white pieces would overwhelm my black troops in next to no time. She was always white, and she always won.

It didn't bother me though, being beaten by Anna, and she'd lend me her books. Mostly, they were girls' schools stories at first, and, the truth is, I wasn't too interested after that. I liked girls' schools stories, but I wouldn't tell anyone! Especially not my friend Jimmy Conroy. Jimmy didn't know that I read anything other than the comics that he gave me.

Jimmy wasn't well-off or anything, but he had older brothers, and they looked after him, so that he was able to have stuff like comics and plastic soldiers that he could lend to me, and that, when I left them alone for ten minutes, Agnes could melt in the fire. When he asked me about them, and I told him that I'd lost them, he said, "Oh!" that's all, just "Oh!" And he never mentioned them again. Jimmy was my friend.

Another good thing about being Jimmy's friend was that you didn't get a lot of hassle in school. You'd get a few beatings from the teachers, of course, but other than that you were mostly left alone. It wasn't just that he was probably bigger and stronger than nearly everyone else in our class, he was older too. He'd been "kept back" twice. Not because he was anyway stupid but, as he'd explained to me, because he just wasn't interested. And one of his brothers was 'Stone Mad' Mickey Conroy, who tore around on motorbikes, and had friends with tattoos and rough-looking faces.

Jimmy was great at football and running, and any other sport that he might try too. He would have been in all the local teams, if he'd had a mind to. Not like me: I was useless, although it wasn't that often that anyone said it to me, on account of my being Jimmy's friend. I don't know what it was that he saw in me!

Everyone liked Jimmy, except for Kate, and Agnes, of course. Kate didn't like him at all, and she said that as he'd been reared in a "den of iniquity," he could never be anything but a bad influence on me. I couldn't have agreed less! To me, Jimmy was the only good influence I'd ever had. Without him, I'd be a complete laughing stock. I wouldn't know how to play conkers, or marbles, or fire a "gat": Jimmy could make great "gats" from tree branches and elastic bands, and then we'd set up bottles and shoot stones at them, although I usually missed. Also, Jimmy, to the best of my knowledge, had always lived with his family on our road, and, anyway, "den of iniquity" sounded like something religious, and Kate was usually into things religious.

Kate was so religious that she went to the church every

chance she got, even when it was raining, and it wasn't a Sunday or some saint's birthday. We were all very religious too, because she made us go with her. The exception being when she had to go to work, and then I'd slip down to Jimmy's, and Anna stayed at home. Agnes wouldn't tell, because she'd have sneaked off somewhere else too.

Kate was so religious that she even had a priest call regularly to the house, to see how she was "coping," he'd say. He was young, thin and dislikeable, and he waved his long, clammy hands at you whenever he spoke. According to Agnes, he had clammy feet as well, because, she said, she could smell them in the room after he'd left. As a rule, I didn't go in there afterwards, but I did take her word for something, for once.

I actually saw more of him than Anna or Agnes, because even though Kate sent us all upstairs when he arrived, I was generally hauled back down again when he was leaving, so that he could confuse me by telling me how Kate was, it seemed, hobbling around with a pile of crosses on her back, and that I had, without being asked to, climbed up on top of them, as if I thought I had a right to or something, and that only for Kate having such a massive Christian, or was it a specifically Catholic, heart beating inside her, she wouldn't be able to support them at all. It was usually stuff like that.

For my part, I think what he wanted, was for me to get off her back, and to take a few of the crosses with me, and then if I ever, although, apparently, I wouldn't unless I did the right exercises, developed a decent pair of proper, manly shoulders, I was to lend her one to lean on. I think he wanted me to carry Anna and Agnes on the other one!

Other times, though, he went on about how I had to guard against the demons that had infested the black souls of my father and mother. Kate reckoned that it was already too late, but he reassured her by telling her that there was always hope, and reminding her of how blessed she had been to be given such a fine pair of daughters. That actually surprised me when I heard it first, because, even in the early days, I'd thought that he had Agnes figured out. I mean, it was only Anna that he smiled at if he caught them around.

Anyway, it must have been that Kate got to coping very badly, because instead of calling, maybe, about once a month, it developed to the stage where he was calling about three times weekly. Sometimes he even called when Kate wasn't expecting him, so that she'd get really flustered, not having had the chance to fix her hair or straighten her lipstick, or whatever else it was she did before he arrived, and then we'd see his big, gangly, purple-faced, pock-marked shape outside and she'd shout at us, in a whisper, to pick this up or throw that out, oftentimes, Anna's teen magazines, that she was reading since she was about seven, and then to clear "the fuck" out of her way.

But, thankfully, there came a time when Kate was able to relax again: He stopped calling. He'd been sent to Africa on "the missions," we were told. To sort out more black souls, I supposed!

Agnes said that he'd had "the hots" for Aunt Kate, but I didn't know what that meant.

* * *

I didn't know that Herbert was arriving until the evening before he did. I heard, or, at least, I overheard, afterwards that Kate had known for ages, but, for whatever reason, she didn't tell us. In fact, she didn't tell me at all! We were sitting around the table having our tea, when she said to Anna and Agnes:

"Your cousin Herbert is coming to stay with us for a while."

Now, I couldn't say that I understand the biology involved, but I didn't consider Herbert to be my cousin. In truth, I didn't, at that time of my life, consider Herbert at all, he being nothing more to me than a far-off rumour. Or, if you prefer, I doubted his existence. Then Kate said "tomorrow," and "his brother," as if it was all my fault, spraying some jammy bread in my direction as she spoke, just in case there was any confusion, I assumed.

I wasn't one for dramatic reactions; I hadn't been brought up that way! I didn't nearly fall off my chair, or molest Aunt Kate with hugs and kisses, or shout "Yahoo!" or even punch the air. I just reached for my own piece of bread and jam, and felt my face flush red.

Agnes filled the vacuum: "No way Ma, you can't be serious! Not him! Jenny told me he stayed up at there place for ages ... they couldn't get rid of him! Why do you want him here Ma?"

"He's family," Kate said, " And anyway," she said, "we need the money."

"He wont have any money," Agnes pleaded, "Jenny told me! He just hangs around the house all day, and then prowls the streets at night. He's a bleedin' spacer Ma!"

Kate, as was her way, reached over and slapped her palm across Agnes face: "I wont have that language in this house!" she bawled. "Herbert's family and I don't give a fuck what your cousin says, that little trollop is full of lies anyway. If it's any of your business, and it's not, your Uncle Jimmy is giving him a start in his yard. As long as he's here, he'll pay for his keep."

But Agnes, always being too stupid to be deterred by physical pain, went on: "Jenny said the corner shop was broken into and the Guards called to their house to talk to him, and then he brought their little Tommy off one day, and all the neighbours were out looking for them because they didn't come back till real late, and Tommy wouldn't tell them where they'd been, and they weren't going to ask HIM! And the dog next- door ran away, and Aunty D's cats would jump of the chairs and starting hissing when he came in, and their grass turned yell ..."

"Stop it!" Kate screamed, "he's coming here tomorrow, and that's it!"

I couldn't wait!

* * *

I couldn't sleep. It was just like before I went back to school after the summer holidays. I lay there trying to think the thoughts that I liked to think when I went to bed at night, but they wouldn't happen.

I couldn't stick with anything; not wars; nor football matches; nor races that I was winning; not even, and it was my favourite one of that period: being chased by a western posse, then taking cover behind a rock on a hillside, my horse having bolted, with only a drop of water left in my canteen to protect against the broiling sun, until Jimmy came riding up to help and we fought it out together. The best I could manage, was to have Herbert, himself, arrive first, and then, single handedly, because I was plum out of bullets as well, save the day.

But even that was far from satisfying, because I had no picture of him. There I was, kneeling behind a rock, protected by an unseen entity who banished my enemies with but a sweep of his invisible six-guns. In the same way, the excitement that was keeping me awake was based on a brother who left the foot-path and the bus-seat empty beside me, as we'd head off on our adventures to be.

Agnes came cackling up the stairs, with Anna telling her to: "Sssh!" She really did cackle. "Ha Ha Ha" in anyone else's language, was "Ca Ca Ca" in hers. Their extra hour must have passed! That gave way then to a low mumbling and tittering as they passed my door; the one advantage I had for being the sole male inhabitant. I didn't have to stretch myself to imagine what might be amusing her: sex! With Agnes it was always sex.

Agne's tongue, if not yet any other part of her, was already notorious in the area. If, when she was with her "friends", a male passed them by who wasn't completely geriatric, deformed, or otherwise incapable, and who wasn't somebody's father that she knew, and that's just giving her the benefit of the doubt, in most cases, she would, likely, shout after him: "Would ye look at the balls on yer man!"or, "Gis a ride there Mister, will ye?" Although he never did; no one with any sense would touch Agnes!

Cocky O' Cleary, his mother might have called him Cormac, not many were sure, didn't have any sense. It was my Aunt Bridgit again, she of the big mouth, who broke the news to Kate. "I refuse to believe that!" came to me so strong, that it pulled me down the stairs and pressed me against the sitting-room door. "I cannot believe that!" Kate thundered again, before I got there.

"But," Bridgit was saying, "It's true. She was seen with him, and them heading into the park!"

"No daughter of mine," Kate swore, "would have anything to do with a drunken, lecherous idiot like him, and anyway he's old enough to be her father."

She was right about Cocky being a drunken idiot, and, although I wasn't sure what lecherous meant, I knew that he followed young girls. As for his age, with his wizened face, and his grey, stubbly beard, we, Jimmy and me, that is, had put him as old as about thirty.

It was before my time, of course, but, seemingly, his mother and father had died and left him not just their house, but enough money to get drunk on as often as he wanted to, so that, as I'd heard someone say, probably Bridgit again, he could forget what he was. I think he followed young girls because older ones didn't like him, or his suit that he'd worn for ten years, with the shirt that was black on the collar and white on the rest of it, or his talons for fingernails, or his speech impediment (Or was that just the drink?), or the way he blew his nose with his fingertips, or his habit of pissing on the footpath at two o' clock in the afternoon. I still thought, though, that he could have done better than Agnes.

Although, I'd heard Kate, and even Bridgit, who both claimed to have known him since he was a kid, say how they felt sorry for him, and that he was harmless, until he was seen near their kids, and then people like Jimmy, Bridgit's husband, threatened to break his legs, and came close to it at least once or twice: Jimmy, and his brother Mickey, found him on the green one night, with his face covered in blood, and he clutching his broken teeth.

Truth was, the young girls were mostly frightened of him, and stayed well away, apart from Agnes, that is." Hey Cocky!" she'd shout at him, staggering up the street, "Do you want to see my tits?" or, "What's the matter with you Cocky, are you not feelin' yourself today? Give us a few bob and I'll do it for you!"

But I didn't know that she had done! And simple-minded and desperate as Cocky might be, I was shocked that he'd let her.

Kate was roaring now: "Get out of my house you carrier of filth, you creature from the gutter, you muck-raker, you

gossip-monger, you snob, you slut, you chinny-faced bitch ..."
You person that's exceeding quick to leave a house when told
to! Because Kate hadn't even warmed up, when Bridgit flew
passed me and out of the door with purpose, and I, having
stepped back out of her way, was pulled forward by Kate who,
vexed as I'd made her, kneed me so hard in the groin, that
when she asked me, "What the fuck," I was doing there, I
wasn't able to explain. Then pushed me into the wall, in a way
that I thought that my nose must be broken – I was wrong,
but it was a bit messy for a few days – threw me on the
floor, kicked me in the stomach, and said: "If I ever catch you
listening at a door again I'll kill you!" I lay there for a while
then listening to her "Aaagnes!" diminish down the street.

She didn't kill Agnes! I was still in the bathroom pouring
cold water on my face, and trying to push toilet roll up my
nose, when I heard the two of them coming in. "I should
never have paid any heed to that bitch of an Aunt of yours,"
Kate was saying, and "I was worse to believe a word of it."
And, in between times, I could hear Agnes say: " I swear Ma,
I wouldn't go near an aul fella like that!" and, "Jesus Ma, how
could you even think ... ?"

Anyway, Kate and Bridgit were back together again now too,
so Herbert was alright for his job with Uncle Jimmy when he
arrived.

* * *

I slept a bit, then I went to school for about a month. I
came home and looked at the clock at half-past three, and
at twenty three minutes to four, then again two days later, at
four o'clock. At half past four, he was due at five, Agnes and
her crew dragged me from the house and, using their skipping

ropes, tied me swiftly, but painfully, they were expert, by my wrists and ankles, backwards to the crossbars of the low garden gate. And then, just in case I might have retained any notion of dignity, or comfort, doused me with a bucketful of icy water.

My only hope was, that he would be delayed! Kate would be home around six, so Agnes would have to release me before then. Anna couldn't help; she was doing something after school. She never said what, but I suspected that she had a boyfriend, even back then, although I still couldn't figure out who he was.

Thankfully, we lived in a pokey cul-de-sac so, at least, I wasn't on view to the general public. Although, that plus was also a minus: our near neighbours already being accustomed to seeing me trussed up in a variety of positions, they weren't going to be to too perturbed by my latest plight. And, anyway, they were all afraid of Agnes!

At least, it showing signs of the beginning of summer, I was drying of fast. But Agnes was more powerful than the weather gods! At what must have been about ten minutes to the hour, I was shouting after her: "You horrible wagon!" as she laughed her way back indoors with another empty pail. "Aaah poor little fella," she sniggered, "did he piddle himself again? Isn't it just as well that big brother'll be along to mind him soon."

It was true: I didn't mind so much getting my hair wet, but this time most of the damage was done to my lower ends. I cursed after her that she'd "die screaming," but it didn't seem to bother her how she died; she just went back to laughing, and sticking her tongue out at me through the open window.

All I could hope for now was that, maybe, Herbert's train was derailed, or that his ship had sunk (No one had said it, but I'd assumed that he'd be crossing water!). Not that

I wished him any harm, of course, because I knew that he'd survive! Or, that he might have been detained by the customs, or even by the police, but only on suspicion of something that he'd be quickly found innocent of, and that wouldn't delay him getting here any later than, say, just a bit after six.

They had me positioned too in such a way that I wouldn't be able to see him coming. Other than the house, all that I had a clear view of, when turning my head to the right, were the innards of our cul-de-sac. And to my left, where lay the main road, my view was obscured by a neighbour's over-hanging hedge. The best I could do, and that was just to try and avoid Agne's leering face, was to swing myself backwards, our gate never shut properly, and hang quietly over the footpath. That's how he found me. Or did he?

I didn't hear him approach; it was more like he just suddenly materialised beside me. And I needn't have been so distressed, because, with neither look nor comment, he just glided past the gate, paying me about as much attention to me as he might to a cheap decoration upon it, and up to the front door and knocked. I didn't say anything either, trying as I was to make myself invisible. My eyes were all that had moved, but enough to see that he was tall, wore a black leather jacket, beneath a khaki coloured rucksack, blue jeans and a pair of boots of a light-coloured hue, that looked as if they wouldn't make much noise wherever they went.

What made me stir though, and almost betray my position, was the hat that he wore. It was a cowboy hat! But not one of those hard, narrow things that John Wayne, or someone like that, might have worn, in the western film's that I watched, but a loose, floppy, black affair, with a kind of white beading around the base of it, and a wide, wide brim. Now, on someone else it might have looked ridiculous, but on him, even from the back, you could see that it was totally cool!

Agnes playing her usual games, he had to knock twice. She answered then, and leaning against the door with her arms folded, and her jaws pumping on the lump of gum wedged between them, she looked him up and down, blew a bubble, allowed it to burst over her lips, pushed it back into her mouth with her filthy fingertips, and declared: "Me ma's not in," and "in anyways, we don't want any!"and made to close the door again.

She didn't succeed! Herbert, defying the physical realities, somehow, magically, slipped in past her fleshy frame and carelessly mounted the stairs. Agnes stood there, trance-like, staring after him. I could hear her "friends" giggling from the room. I laughed too. She'd never forgive him for that. She wouldn't forgive me either!

* * *

Surprisingly, and thankfully, Anna missed the fun by only about fifteen minutes. I supposed, like myself, she couldn't wait to meet him. It was for me, though, a fairly uncomfortable time, in that, not only did I get soaked again, but was swung around on the gate a bit, as well, and whacked on the head with the wooden end of one of the skipping ropes - Agnes was raging! Still, I took it all in my stride; I couldn't really care less now!

Although, when Anna released me and we went inside, we were disappointed to find that he hadn't still stirred from "his room." It was actually my room, but somehow Herbert had known exactly where to find it, Kate having allocated it to him for the duration of his stay. I was to sleep on the floor downstairs, even if I had suggested to her that the floor in my own room would be every bit as comfortable and that, up there, I'd be less in the way. She told me, though, that my comfort, or otherwise, was neither here nor there, and that she didn't want me to be, under any circumstances, bothering Herbert. And anyway, she said, if it did transpire that I became a nuisance downstairs, she was sure that there was plenty of other places where she could put me e.g: orphanages, reform schools, juvenile correctional centres, work-farms, psychiatric hospitals, or wherever else maladjusted kids were sent to in those days, that she regularly threatened me with.

He was still there too when Kate got home from work. But she had the gall to call into him, so that, whatever arrangement they came to, he didn't come down for tea either, and it was already almost dark outside when he finally did appear.

The women were stretched across the furniture, while I cooled my buttocks on the lino floor, through the thin summer shorts that I was still forced to wear (a major source of embarrassment at my age! Although, unbeknownst to Kate, I did keep a pair of "longers" down at Jimmy's). Kate, as was her usual, snored on the couch, while Anna, crouched over a book by the window, tried to utilise the last of the daylight; Kate always insisting that, where possible, we should always favour "God's light" over the man-made sort provided by the Electricity Supply Board. Whereas Agnes was lost in some rubbish on the television, that no-one else would watch. So it was, that I was the first to be aware of his presence.

"How are ye, Herbert," I said, and so quietly that the others mightn't hear. "I'm you're brother Billy!"

"Hello to you too," he replied, taking me comfortably in his stride, and settling himself above Kate's head.

Sitting on the arms of Kate's furniture was strictly forbidden, but I wasn't going to tell him that! But I could get a look at him now: Without the hat, he seemed to have a mop of black hair, and the type of moustache and chinnish-beard set that wouldn't have been at all popular where we came from. In the bad light too, he appeared to have a long nose, which made me wonder if he looked like me. Anna was the first of the girls to spot him. "Hi Herbert," she said, and he, somehow knowing exactly who she was, replied, "Hi Anna."

But Agnes butted in then with more of her faked innocence and, I could tell, real annoyance, I'm sure that he was aware of it too! "Oh Herbert," she lied, "I'm really sorry about earlier, I should have remembered that you were due. It's just that we've had all kinds of other weirdos comin' around here. Kate says that we shouldn't even open the door when she's not here. But anyway," she said, "how are you? Isn't it just great that you're going to be staying with us! Aunty D was tellin' me how much she enjoyed you being with them."

Herbert making no comment, and, again in the gloom, any facial expressions he might have made being indecipherable to me, she went on: "I hope that that room is alright for you? And don't be worrying now that you're putting anyone out, sure isn't it's only little Willie's," she said, indicating me with a kick of her, already sized-seven, platformed-shoe, and then: "How was your journey? Ma said that you came over from England." She hadn't told me!

"Okay," Herbert answered.

"It must cost a fortune to travel over?" she said. "You're probably broke after it?"

"It is," he said

"Though," she said, "I heard that you can make a pile of money over there, workin' on the buildin' or whatever?"

"Is that so?" he replied.

Agnes, of course, couldn't wear a mask of politeness for long, no matter how thin it might have been: "So what were you doin' in England than Herbert? Dossin' was it? Ma tells us that you're plannin' on workin' for Uncle Jimmy, but you'll hardly stick that now, will you Herbert? I mean, what's the story Herbert?"

But Herbert rose, gave a bow and re-fixing his hat (Where did that come from? I hadn't noticed him bringing it in!), said, "I'll catch up with you all later," and calmly made his exit.

If he'd have happened to have looked down, when he was stepping back over me, I'm sure he couldn't but have noticed how much I was admiring him, bent forward as I was, with my hands clasped together, and with my lips muttering his praises. I mean, it was just brilliant; the way that he had tied Agnes up in knots, and then, cool as you like, split the scene.

There was, though, just a little something nagging at me. It was that if he was going to be my saviour, I wanted him to be on site. I mean, what use were the cavalry to the besieged pilgrim, if they just rode up, fired a few shots and then headed off again, leaving the Indians even more incensed? I hoped that wasn't to be the way he would continue. But then, I needn't have worried. I should have realised that he would have other, more mysterious, ways of settling things out.

* * *

I hardly ever say him. He did start with Uncle Jimmy, and the very next day at that. He was gone before we got up in the mornings, wasn't back by tea-time, and then when he did get in, which was usually about seven, ate on his own, Anna or Kate, always having something ready for him. He'd disappear upstairs then, and wouldn't emerge until about nine, on his way out of doors again.

I couldn't get near him! Even if Kate was asleep when he was eating, Agnes guarded the kitchen, and there wasn't a way past her, at all! And whatever hour he returned at night, was too late a one for me, because even though I tried to stay awake and listen, silent traveller that he was, I never heard him coming in. My only contact with him was through his music.

He played it every evening on the record player he'd brought into the room. Most times, when Kate was asleep, I sat outside the door and listened too. There was very little of it that I'd heard before. Up to then, in terms of modern music, I hadn't been exposed to a lot more than the radio pop songs of a sponsored Saturday afternoon, that were, invariably, prematurely halted by the DJ, so that he could extol the virtues of an oat flake, or a cattle vaccine, or bring to us the great news about the latest big thing in slug repellants, and the bits of tunes that wafted through the walls, on nights that I couldn't sleep, from Anna's 'Radio Luxembourg.' Even 'Top of the Pops', for us, had yet to come on stream.

I liked the new sounds, a lot! My eavesdropping stints became the high points of my days. I felt so good up there, that I stopped worrying about being caught, and about school and not having my homework done, even about Agnes. After a while, it didn't even seem that important to meet him in person anymore.

I often wondered who these bands and singers were that made me feel so good. But I couldn't see any way of finding out, other than going into the room, when he wasn't there, and having a look. Which was, as it happened, not that I would have done it anyway, out of the question: He'd gotten a key from Kate, that I didn't know existed, and kept it locked. Not that I blamed him; not with Agnes about. Given the chance she'd surely wreck all his stuff, just out of malice and spite.

One evening, though, he caught me sitting at the top of the stairs, and all I could splutter was: I ... I like the music ... Who's it by?" And, he said, the first time he'd spoken to me since "Hello," and that must have been all of ten days before: "Go in and see." But I didn't; I waited for him to come back from the toilet first.

The room was much the same as I'd left it. The most noticeable difference to it was, indeed, the record player sitting on the chair, that he'd brought up from below, with the records piled against it. My metal, unmeltable, World War Two British infantrymen, as recently conscripted by means of Jimmy's 'Victor' comics, still guarded the windowsill, and my plastic 'Samurai' warriors sword, with the broken blade, still hung alone on the wall; Kate not allowing me any football posters. The Pope and the Virgin Mary, in statuette, were, as always, on the shelf, although with Mary now atop of my 'War Picture Gallery' books; he must have had the window open at some stage. I had no other possessions. His rucksack and a few bits of clothing peeped out from under the bed, but you wouldn't have noticed them, unless you were very curious.

He lay now on the bed and lit a cigarette, so I picked up the nearest sleeve and, it being unoccupied, decided that it belonged to the record that was playing. It was by The Doors, and it was one of my, and his, favourites; he played it a lot. I particularly liked 'The End.' As soon as I'd hear it now, I'd turn off the light on the landing, if it was on, all the better to savour it.

There was more from The Doors, and David Bowie's 'Hunky

Dory.' 'Quicksand' was special, although I couldn't say why. I remembered the guitar playing on 'I heard her call my name,' from amongst the Velvet Underground albums, and Jimi Hendrick's 'All along the Watchtower.' Bob Dylan was there too, but I don't think he was played that much. I took my time over a Mother's of Invention cover, not so much on account of the music, but more that I thought Frank Zappa looked very like Herbert, if only in the facial hair, because I still hadn't a clear picture of him. Even now, when I chanced to look up, his features were clouded in smoke. I was sure, though, that I didn't look like either of them.

Then there was a lot of stuff that I couldn't place at all, including one by someone whose name ended in "sky" and a couple with trumpets on the covers, that I don't think that he listened to much either.

When I'd finished and put them back, as he'd had them, I said, because I couldn't think of anything else to say, "They're really great!"

But, he replied: "It's mostly crap, but it's better than nothing."

So, I just said: "Thanks," and left the room.

He didn't ask me in again, but he didn't need to! I could sit outside now and try and work out who was who, and what was what. And the weather getting better, and my making a few bob cleaning windows with Jimmy, if I could when he asked me to, I was able to enlist some help. Although, the magazines that I bought were mainly occupied by Slade and The Osmonds, so that they ended up, for the most part, on Agnes's wall.

If, and when, I was really confused, and I thought about knocking on Herbert's door, I never actually did so: I hadn't the nerve! I tried to talk to Jimmy about it, but Jimmy wasn't even into Slade. What he did say, though, was that it was very important that I got close to Herbert, just in case that I got into a fight or anything.

* * *

Most times if Herbert was asked a question he'd answer: "I couldn't tell you." Not if someone shouted in to ask him was his tea alright? Or, did he have a good day? Then, he'd say "Fine!" or, more likely, not answer at all, so that by about the third evening, he was left in peace. By all but Agnes, that is, who would always persevere.

Not that she kept shouting into him when he was eating, but that she'd catch him in the hallway or on the stairs afterwards, and we'd hear her say something like, "Well where are you off to again tonight Herbert ... somewhere exciting is it?" And he'd say, "I couldn't tell you!"

So then she'd say something like, "How do you feel about having a snivelling brother like that little rat Willie?" But, again he'd say: "I couldn't tell you!" and walk on by. One time, around then, they told us in school the story about the man who first said that the world wasn't flat, and how he was called mad and, all in all, given a terrible time, and it made me think about Herbert, and his keeping all sorts to himself. One day, though, Anna asked him a question and he answered: "Yes."

It must have been a Sunday, because he wasn't working ,and we were all at home bar Kate. Anna and myself were in the sitting-room playing chess, and she was just finishing me off again, when he passed the open door, and she said, and without any warning to me: "Herbert would you like a game?" I don't know what came over her, but then I shouldn't have been surprised; she had courage, had Anna, she wasn't even afraid of Agnes!

I moved to let him sit down, and then went to find him an ashtray. When I returned, the pieces were all set up and they were ready to start: Anna was poised over her leading pawn, whereas he sat back, with his hat tilted over his eyes. Before Anna made her move though, she asked Agnes to make less noise with her bubble-gum, and for me to shift away a bit from where I'd been kneeling beside him, with my head bowed over the board.

So I stood behind him, with my hands clasped in front of me and my stomach wobbling with nerves, my feet wanting to jig along with it too. I tried my best to stay still, because I didn't want to distract him. But I couldn't, not when Anna's advancing white army took two of his pawns without incurring a casualty of it's own. She had to speak to me again! "Sorry!" I said, bolting my feet to the floor, and strapping my shaking arms across my chest. But, really, I wanted to whisper in his ear: to warn him to be careful, very careful, that Anna was clever, and not just for a girl. And then, when Anna took another one of his pawns, and one of his bishops as well, I wanted to stop the game; maybe feign a collapse, or just, blatantly, upturn the board. But I shouldn't have doubted him!

Immediately, he avenged his black bishop with a white one. His knights charged forwards, and supported by his rooks, laid waste to her front ranks. Her second bishop fell, her knights were toppled, her rooks retreated to protect their ailing queen – he had no need for his – only to be outflanked, and see her taken by his loan marauding bishop. Soon it was all over; his triumphant black troops swarmed over the board, and laid siege to her desolate king.

He rose, thanked Anna, and walked out. I followed in his footsteps, only to be overtaken by Agnes, who said, and loudly enough for him to hear: "I'll find him out; your black bastard!"

* * *

They played chess again, did Anna and Herbert, but I didn't bother watching; I knew who would always win, although I did watch him. On Sunday afternoons, when Kate was out, me in front of the television, he across the room, still with his hat and cigarettes on, so that I wasn't sure that he even looked like Frank Zappa anymore. But I was sure that he didn't look like anyone on our mother's side, that I'd met. Which led me to think that he might look like our father. Until I remembered that there was no 'our father,' only his father and my father, who, incidentally, I'd believed to be, for a while when I was even younger, the Devil's son, and that I was too, and not his grandson! It was Aunt Bridgit, again, who caused my confusion.

I'd been trained to be polite to her when she called. So polite, that on one occasion she complimented Kate on my good manners, but said that she hoped that I wasn't "a changeling like my father." 'A changeling,' sounding interesting, I sought out the dictionary that Anna kept under her bed, and found it defined as: "A child believed to be substituted for another child," which made not a bit of sense to me, at all!

I thought about it long and hard, as long and hard as I could think about anything in those days, but the best I could come up with was that my father wasn't who everyone, apart from Bridgit and maybe a few others in the family, thought that he was. That he wasn't who he seemed to be; he was, in fact, someone else entirely, but what did that mean? And if that was the case, and I was like him, and I wasn't who everyone thought that I was either; that I'd been swopped too, then, surely, he wasn't my father anyway? At times like these, I, also, didn't like Bridgit.

Deciding that dictionaries weren't up to much, I put it to rest, realising that what Bridgit must have really meant was that my father was a master of disguise, like someone of the television, maybe a character from 'Batman' or 'The Man from Uncle,' except that he was even better at it. So I took myself to putting black marker over my upper lip, turning my coat inside out and walking with a distinctive limp. But I didn't fool anyone!

That's how it was, until some time later when Kate got herself involved with a Charismatic Christian group, who even organised meetings for us kids, once weekly.

There were held in the home of a near-neighbour, but Kate made sure to march us up there anyway, and to collect us afterwards. The man in command was a Mr. Ellis Woods, but we called him nothing but "Elijah" (Anna's idea, and she was one of the few that paid any attention to him!), although not to his face, of course.

If "Elijah" wasn't boring us with his readings from the Bible, he was embarrassing us, well speaking for myself anyway, by making us clap, sing and shout "Praise be ..." And, at times like those, it was also, I have to say, very hard for me to concentrate on being pinned down in a trench somewhere by an unseen enemy sniper, until I lifted the dead body of a comrade against the parapet, duping him into betraying his position amidst the far-facing trees, as his flashing muzzle planted another bullet into the corpse, before I took aim and exacted retribution, with but a single shot of my own.

Or, to be holed up in the ruins of a fallen building with

Jimmy beside me, the shells exploding around us, and, through the rubble, our foe advancing stealthily towards us, only, on coming within our range, to fall victims to our unerring precision with our super, multi-purpose, rapid-fire, rocket-launching, grenade throwing, even known on occasion to convert into flying machines, if only suitable for one person's use, machine guns.

But, it was one night, just before we started all that leaping around nonsense, that I heard it; somehow it had extracted itself from all the other words that I was trying not to listen to, and I, and it wasn't like me, spoke up, and asked, "Excuse me sir, but what do you mean by a changeling?"

Elijah rocked backed on his heels (He sang on his toes, like "a real prick with ears,"someone had said – I think it was Agnes!), and answered: "A changeling is a a child of Satan sent to take the place of another."

So now I knew, and I felt really good about it too! Surely as a son of Satan there were lots of incredible things that I could do. So, I developed a sinister laugh and an evil eye, and invoked my "Father" to make bad things happen to people that didn't like me.

But I was to be disappointed: all that happened, was that Kate said that I was developing a facial twitch "along with everything else," and forced me to take some horrible medicine for my bad throat, and Agnes beat me up again. So too did a couple of other kids, who didn't know that I was a friend of Jimmy's.

Although, that was as bad as it got, because I was, surprisingly, saved from any worse by another visit from Bridgit, who, I overheard, tell Kate how Richard, her son, was becoming a 'Veritable Adonis.' Curious again, this time I went directly to Anna who, at about age eleven, was able to tell me that a

'Veritable Adonis' was an "exceedingly handsome Greek god."
So, I thought about Richard and his spots and his greasy hair,
and he almost as puny as I was, and I realised that, yes, indeed,
I was truly not the son of Satan!

But Herbert, maybe he was a real changeling?

* * *

Jimmy Conroy's mother had left him too, maybe that was what
he saw in me? Jimmy's mother ran off with the milkman, like
in a joke on the television, and it was in our neighbourhood,
although an old one that wasn't told that much anymore,
except by the likes of Agnes, who'd made sure to tell me as
soon as I was old enough to get it.

I had known before that Jimmy's mother had gone, but not
of the circumstances. Like me, with my own, he had no real
memory of, and rarely mentioned her. I suppose, to be honest,
the way I was thinking at the time that I heard it – six months,
maybe, before Herbert? – what really intrigued me was the
obvious truth in the stories about the erotic adventures of
milkmen. So, I pictured our own with his frosty face and his
blemished fingers, and him rattling his bottles at half five in
the morning, and put it down as a possible career choice.

Jimmy's house wasn't always a mess! His father, 'The
Scotchman,' didn't do a lot more than drink, but there was
another brother, older than Jimmy and younger than Mickey,
who cleaned a lot, and did the cooking too, his name was
Patrick: Not Pat; nor Paddy; nor even Patsy; but always
Patrick!

If Jimmy or Mickey had caught someone else, like me, for
instance, doing the same, they would have given him an awful
slagging, but Patrick wasn't called a "Nancy Boy," or a "Fairy,"

when he did the housework. I suppose, if he had been, they would have starved.

I liked to be in that house, even when Jimmy's father woke up shouting and ordering everyone out. Or, told us again about how he could have played for "Celtic."

He really was Scottish, Jimmy's father, and when he was still, "a wee bit wet behind the ears," he was approached after a junior football game by a representative from the famous Glasgow club, who said, and these were his very words: "Son, what a talent you have," and, "It'll be a tragedy if you don't play for your country some day," and set about making arrangements for him to meet his boss.

But before Jimmy's father gained the acquaintance of the great man, grave fortune overtook him: His girlfriend fell pregnant, and he, being the man that he was, felt honour-bound to marry and return with her, and the unborn Mickey, to her Dublin homeplace. It was indeed a tragedy, and not just for Scotland.

It has to be said that, when he was a bit sober, he liked to have a kick about on the road with Jimmy and myself, and that you could tell, if you knew anything at all about football, that even with his baldy head, and his belly hanging out over the front of his trousers, that he was class.

"Waa d'ye tink o' da son?" he'd say, when you stood there in awe looking at him go past you again, and him hardly out of breath. Although, I couldn't agree with Jimmy when he said that he might still play for Scotland: he told me that he was thirty-one or two, and that was ancient!

You didn't see Jimmy's brother Mickey much; he'd be out on his motorbike. He'd only got a small one at the time, but you could tell that he was going to get himself a really massive one by the studded leather gear and the helmet with all the stickers on it that he wore. If he was in, he was usually looking at one of his bike magazines, the floor'd be littered with them. Sometimes in the winter, or maybe even in the summer, Jimmy's father would use them to light the fire. There'd be war!

I was there for one of them: Mickey called his father, "a useless washed up slob," and, "a drunken good-for-nothing," so that his father, who was also called Mickey, by the way, got up off the floor, grabbed him by the collar and said: "Get oot, get oot, ye ungrateful wee git, and dinnae come back nae more, nae more." But they didn't mean it: they were back together within the hour.

Jimmy said that Mickey would never be thrown out because of all the money that he earned, and that he himself was going to leave school soon and get a job too.

Patrick often moved the magazines, but nobody said a word.

* * *

I wasn't the only regular caller to Conroy's. Mickey, of course, had his friends too, and then there was Rory Brophy; or 'Roly' Brophy as he was known. I didn't know what Jimmy saw in him either!

When he squinted at you with those beady eyes, and that sneaky sneer on his face, you knew that he was thinking: "I'm better than you. I'm cuter than you are. I'll be here for just as long as it suits me to be, but when I'm accepted elsewhere, I'll have no more to do with the likes of you or your Jimmy." He was allowed out a lot more than me though, and he stuck to Jimmy like the leech that he was.

He never brought cigarettes, and when we played poker a lot in the summer, with the money we got from cleaning the windows, he didn't lose, or, at least, nothing worth mentioning. When he was "down" no more than a couple of pence, he'd stand up, and say: "Well that's me ... I'm off!" Which might have been okay, except that he tried it when he was winning too. As if we didn't notice!

The worst of it though, was that Jimmy would let him go. He'd just say, "Okay so," as if he didn't realise what was happening. I always meant to speak to him about it, but I never did, I suppose, because I'd never go against Jimmy. Roly even tried it once when Mickey and a friend were playing, but Mickey's mate said: "Hey fat boy get back in that seat!" and that was the end of that!

Mickey and his friends didn't play that often, which might have been a good thing, because they always made me a bit nervous when they did.

Roly rarely cleaned windows, he'd only do it if Jimmy was really stuck; he didn't have to, he always had money anyway. He lived close by, but his family were well off, everyone knew that! They had a shiny car and a garden full of ornaments, and his mother, when it wasn't raining, polished her brass door-knob and got her hair done outside of the area. Neither did she go to the bingo with the rest of them, but let everyone know about the 'Bridge' club, where she was a member. She only let Roly out so much, because she thought that he'd be with his "nice" friends from the new school that she'd moved him to. He wouldn't dare tell her that he'd been down at Jimmy's!

Jimmy's father didn't like him either. I heard him say that there were "no flies on yer man," and he didn't tell him his story like he did the rest of us. Most of all though, Jimmy's father didn't like women. "Donnae ever get married, son," he'd say, "they'll take your very soul and never give it back to ye." And it was just as well that none of his sons, not even

Mickey, were bothered with steady girlfriends, because often he'd wake up roaring: "Ye can keep yer bloody husseys out o' my hoos!"

And it wasn't just indoors that he did his shouting; he'd often stand at the gate and demand of people "what the friggin fuck they were lookin' at?" and ask them if they never saw "a broken man" before, and then curse them generally in Scottish.

No one paid much heed to him. Even Cocky was too busy being drunk on the other side of the street to pay a lot of attention. Some of the men passing by did say "hello," and some even said that didn't they know how it is; as if it was just the same for them! They didn't stop though. They never stopped. Except for Herbert: Herbert stopped!

Agnes came running in one day, red in the face with excitement. "Guess who's just been talking to mouldy Mickey?" she said. There were further sightings too.
I wondered what it was that they spoke of. One day, when Jimmy's father was on his own, apart from me, that is, I said to him, and I knew it was the type of underhand tactic that I must have picked up from Agnes: "Herbert tells me that he's been talkin' to you?"

But, he answered: "Son, did I ever tell ya that I coulda' played for Celtic?"

Another time though, he said to me: " Son, your brother's a lord."

"Our Lord!" I answered.

* * *

Agnes had become obsessed with Herbert. She was at the end of her tether. He had to be the first person that she'd ever encountered whom she couldn't intimidate; even at school she was reputed to have made broken wrecks of the toughest of teachers. But with him, it still went on!

Question: "What do you think Herbert?" As in, what do you think Herbert, about people allowing their kids out at night when there's strange characters lurking about?
Answer: "I couldn't say!"

Question: "Where do you go Herbert?" As in, over to the park is it, to hang around the trees in the hope that you might meet up with some poor, lost soul?

Answer: "I couldn't tell you!"

And then, when he'd breezed on by, she'd resorted to saying: "Fuckin' weirdo!" Resorted to saying it to him, that is; she'd bleated it in everyone else's ear since before he'd even arrived, even citing the incident of his by-passing her at the doorstep, to all who she made listen to her, as evidence of his depravity: "The bollocks just went right through me!" and warning them to stay well clear of him, and to advise their kinsfolk to do the same.

She wasn't afraid to voice her opinion to Kate either, if she thought she could get away with it, or, more likely, when her humour was so foul that she just couldn't help herself, then she'd say: "He's a fuckin' mentler Ma!" But Kate would tell her to shut her, "big, ugly mouth," and remind her of how grateful she should be to have Herbert with us, and him contributing so generously to the household budget, unlike other useless males, whom she could mention by name, if she'd wanted to, who hung around the house, forever under her feet, and weren't even worth the good food that she fed them.

But Agnes would persist: "But Ma, he's a fuckin' madman, everyone knows that! He doesn't even speak to anyone that's normal. He gives me the creeps, he does."

Usually then, Kate would threaten her with violence, not that it wasn't noticeable that she was increasing reluctant to use it, probably in recognition of the worrying fact that Agnes was fast becoming more adept at it than she was herself. Still and all, Agnes would do a Herbert then, and not talk to anyone either, not even Anna, who she'd also accused of being a weirdo. Although, only for nothing like permanent, and then Anna would be the first to be pardoned, her co-operation being required for the successful completion of various household chores, and Agnes's homework.

It has to be said though, that there was, generally, a markable reduction in our incidence of domestic violence. Apart from Kate's containing of herself, if only with Agnes, Agnes herself was less inclined to "wipe that fuckin smile" of my face, when aware of Herbert's presence; he really did give her "the creeps."

Although, there were, of course, still times when she just couldn't control herself. But then, Agnes could destroy you just with her attitude: It was like she had this atmosphere inside her, that she could release whenever she wanted to. All she had to do, to summon it up, was fold her arms across her chest, press her lips together and make a "TTT" sound with her tongue. Then it filled the room and made you tense and edgy, and incapable of enjoying the television programme that you were watching. Or, it spilled over your dinner, and left the food tasting rotten and your stomach sick when you swallowed it. It even worked out of doors; the air then got so clammy that your head felt heavy and your legs wobbled, when you had to go somewhere with her and Aunt Kate.

Thankfully though, Herbert was totally immune to it, because when she called him a "fuckin' weirdo" again, and he just said: "Maybe," she unleashed a load of it at him, before storming out of the house, and all the way to Uncle Jimmy's.

It was Bridgit who related the story: Apparently, Agnes had had herself, breathlessly, escaping Herbert's manic clutches, and told tales of Uncle Jimmy's timber yard being filled at night by gangs of crazies who worshipped the Devil and did strange things to children, and small animals too. She even tried convicting him of various larcenies unsolved in the area. But Uncle Jimmy wasn't convinced: he wouldn't sack him!

There were others, though, who were. Agnes was a genius when it came to spreading vicious rumour: She could cross herself and swear on anyone's life, usually on Kate's or Anna's, say, so impressively, that you'd believe her, if you didn't know that she actually didn't give a shit about anyone!

Woman now crossed the street on Herbert's approach. Kid's screamed for their mammies. Pets were kept indoors. The local clergy preached caution of mysterious interlopers.

She was bad, that Agnes one.

* * *

She was very curious too, was Agnes, and as she had no legitimate means of finding out what it was that Herbert really got up to of an evening, neither her nor her cronies being allowed out after dark, she devised an alternative means of satisfying her longing. She mentioned it to Anna: "I'm goin' t' find out what the fuck he's up to," she said.

I knew that it was about him that she was speaking because, apart from her using her low, hard-done-by, but will-get-even-with-him-yet tone, that she'd developed when when she spoke about Herbert, she didn't march across the room, grab me by the neck, and say: " Well Willie, what the fuck's goin' on then?"

I was fortunate to have heard her. I only did so, because the news had come on television: five minutes earlier, and I would have been totally caught up in the latest adventure of 'Pippi Longstocking,' the girl that did all those magic things. But I didn't pay much attention to the news, as it was usually just about the Catholics and the Protestants up North killing each other. All because of the "Virgin Mary," Kate had once said. But I couldn't relate to that at all; I didn't know anyone who didn't believe in the Virgin Mary like I did, not even when I found out what a Virgin Mary was.

It wasn't the kind of war that I could have gotten into anyway: There was hardly any crouching behind shattered buildings, and little or no chasing down narrow streets throwing hand grenades after a fleeing enemy. On the way home from school then, we used to sing, to the air of, I think, a New Seekers song, that the Brits might have entered in the Eurovision Song Contest:

> "I'd like to join the IRA
> and furnish it with guns
> grow gelignite and dynamite
> and blow up the British bums"

But I didn't really mean it! Leaving a bomb in "an abandoned car" or in "an arcade crowded with shoppers," couldn't have been very exciting. I would have been much more interested in a war like the one that the Americans had with the Vietnamese, with plenty of jungle fire-fights and wading through swamps with a rifle over your head. Except for the snakes and flesh-devouring creatures – I wouldn't have been into them at all! And I was "up" for the Vietnamese. But we didn't get to see a lot of that war, because of the one in the North.

So, Agnes said to Anna: "I'm goin' t' find out what the fuck he's up to," and, "I'm goin' to follow him tomorrow night when me Ma's at the bingo." And it was easy for me to pick-up on the bones of Agne's scheme; her voice always rose when she thought she was being clever, or smart.

It was, as I expected, a very simple plan: So that Kate wouldn't believe anyone who might spot her out, Agnes was going to feign illness and take to her bed before Kate departed. Then after exposing Herbert, as she was convinced that she would do, and in the likely event that she didn't get back before Kate did, having made sure to leave the side-gate unbolted, she would sneak out the back and pitch pebbles at her and Anna's window, whereupon Anna, having kept a wakeful vigil, would slip downstairs and gain her entry.

I knew that Anna, in principle, wouldn't have agreed with this blatant prying into Herbert's private doings, but I did understand that she was motivated by the need to clear any wrongful suspicions of him from the minds of Agnes, and all the others that she had tarnished. She even had her own ideas on Agnes' plan, although they had to have been influenced by the amount of schoolgirl stories that she had read.

Apart from pushing pillows under Agnes' bedclothes, so that in the, unprecedented, event of Kate making a late night surveillance, she would be assured that everyone was where they should be, Anna had also suggested, that, for discretion's sake, Agnes should, on return, approach, not head-on, but from the laneway behind us. Then after climbing the back wall, she would, after alerting Anna, regain her chamber by pulling herself up the line of sheets that Anna would have knotted together, secured to a bed-leg and draped out the window.

I could have choked, and not out of anger anymore. It was just as well that neither of them happened to look my way, because I would have had a hard job convincing them that I was sniggering at the latest carnage on the television, although Agnes might have done!

What had me quivering and clutching my sides, was the thought that if Enid Blyton, or anyone else whose books Anna used to read, had had someone scaling walls and hauling themselves up sheets in the middle of the night, it most certainly wouldn't have been a hulk such as Agnes. Neither would she have cast lathlike Anna in the role of sole helper.

For someone so bright, Anna could be very stupid at times. But to be fair, she had a sense of humour too. The action couldn't happen soon enough for me. But I was to be disappointed!

* * *

I fell asleep. I don't know how I did, but I fell asleep! Kate went to the bingo, Herbert went out, Agnes followed, Kate came home again, and then I fell asleep.

I'd sat up watching the late film with Anna. We did that on a Friday night when Kate went to bingo, because win, lose, or draw, she was sure to go for a drink afterwards, and wouldn't be home until about midnight.

The film was of that supernaturally, spine-chillery, late-night type, that compelled you to watch because of the warnings beforehand of their unsuitability for nervous viewers. Although, mostly they disappointed, which was probably a good thing, because if you were a genuinely nervous viewer, then you mightn't have a lot of options, probably still having only the one TV channel, unless, of course, you were old enough and could go out to the pub with Kate and her mates, other than risking a breakdown.

As far as I can recall, it wasn't up to much: it was just the usual run-of-the-mill sort of production, that concerned itself with tortured souls languishing in the Netherworld, who put the fear of God into honest folk, particularly good-looking young women, who screamed terribly, until relieved by an intrepid and handsome hero. Any ugly-looking ones, it seemed, were left to their horrible fates!

But then again, if it had been the greatest film ever made, with absolutely loads of violence and naked women's breasts, it, probably, would have been wasted on me that night. Anna was the same; she kept fidgeting in her chair, and walking up and down the stairs, or footering with the newspaper in her lap. But the film ending, and the National Anthem playing, she stood up, turned it off and headed for bed. I settled down with a comic and waited. Although, I didn't pay my 'Hornet' much attention that night.

I could hear Anna moving about upstairs; to and from the window, I supposed, waiting for sight or sound of Agnes. She wasn't tying her sheets together, she done that already; I'd sneaked into her room and checked! Sometimes I worried about Anna, in spite of her sense of humour, and I was very concerned about her now.

Apart from her getting into trouble with Kate, she might injure herself! I could picture the bed flying towards the window with her helplessly astride it, or the anchor leg collapsing beneath it. But, worst of all, I could see a panicking Agnes grasping her fragile arm and flinging her critically earthwards.

I considered warning her, even offering to help, but then I wouldn't have liked her to think that I'd been listening in on her conversations, even if they were only with Agnes: Already, she'd had the idea that I'd been hanging around her bedroom door, and looking through the keyhole whilst she was getting undressed, but only until I'd convinced her that I'd dropped something out there – twice! Agnes had accused me too, but that was just jealousy!

I tried to console myself with Kate's dictum that if Anna insisted on living in a fantasy world, it was only right and proper, and in her best interests that, like me, she'd find out the "the hard way." Even if, in her case, she was unlikely to suffer as many abrasions and contusions along the road, she would, as with myself, still have to "pull her head out of the clouds," and "get her feet back on the ground," that is, if she ever wanted to "rejoin the human race". And, if she wanted to "get on in this life," even if it was just to "put food on the table," and get a "roof over her head," she'd have to "keep her head down," and "stick to the straight and narrow," and, maybe, to her "guns," as well. She might even have to "be her own man." But if she insisted on having her head "filled with foolishness," she'd just have to "suffer the consequences," and they, apparently, didn't "bear thinking about".What were they, the consequences? Anyway, she'd have to "get a grip of herself," and "pull herself together," otherwise ... otherwise? I hadn't learned, but Anna would be a lot quicker on the uptake.

But I was still trying to console myself, when Kate got in, made a cup of tea and went to bed. Then it was morning.

* * *

Anna was shaking me, and shouting -Kate must have gone to work already-: "Get up, Billy! Get up!" She must have been at it for a while before I was aware of it, because my head was pounding, and I didn't get headaches in those days! I was very tired too.

"Get up! Get up, you lazy bastard!" she said, letting me know how stressed she was, because Anna wouldn't call me that. "Get up! Get up! We've got to find her!" I'd left her no option but to pull me by the few hairs that protruded from the top of my sleeping bag, my having zipped it so tightly to put the rest of me, to her, inaccessible.

"Okay, okay," I said, and slowly started to reveal myself.

It wasn't often that I got the opportunity of exposing myself to Anna and, bad and all as I was feeling, I was determined to make the most of it: I let her have a bit of bare arm and shoulder first, then a bit of chest, before sliding out my middling bits, hoping that the stained, holey Y-Fronts that I was wearing didn't take completely from there appeal.

But I needn't have bothered; Anna didn't show the slightest sign of interest. In fact, she was back staring at the walls again. So, I said: "What's the matter?" and, "What's the story?" and, "Fill us in, will you? and, when she still didn't answer, "Where's the fire?" a fashionable thing to say, back then. That brought her around; she told me everything that I knew, plus a bit that I didn't: "He came back,"she said, "but she didn't."

Maybe, I suggested, that Agnes, not being able to climb the back wall, had found herself a comfortable spot and was still asleep in a neighbour's garden.

No, Anna replied, she'd kept a check all night, and if Agnes had, at any stage, been in the laneway, she would have known about it.

Maybe, I suggested, that Agnes, unaware of the hour, and having lost her nerve regarding the sheets, was still wandering the streets waiting for Kate to exit.

No, Anna replied, she'd already gone out and looked around, and there wasn't a sign of her. And, anyway, she said, Agnes had taken Kate's old watch with her.

Maybe, I suggested, that a flying saucer landing in the area and crewed not by the usual type of life-forms, but by a renegade band of brain-dead morons, cast from their planet for crimes against nature, had taken her aboard as a fine example of young earthling womanhood.

No, Anna replied, those craft that were now being referred to as 'Unidentified Flying Objects' were, apparently, as yet, unlikely to land near population centres, preferring to take their humanoid samples from outback dwellers and desert warriors. Also, she said, that it was believed that those same craft had little or no autonomy, their movements being ordained by a programme of the 'Great Central Computer,' so that even if one did fall into the hands of a band of brain-dead renegades, it's range would be totally limited. Furthermore, she said, that there were those who believed that even the thought patterns and the decision-making faculties of the denizens of these craft were controlled by the self-same computer, so that he who saw himself as the greatest rebel was, in fact, doing no more than acting out a role for the benefit of the greater purpose. And, anyway, she said, as far as Agne's possible selection was concerned, they were only interested in males at the moment.

I couldn't think of anything else to suggest then - I felt lousy! I wished she'd just leave me, so that I could go back to sleep, but she wouldn't.

"You'd better go over to the park," she said, "and look there. She could have fallen into a ditch and broken her leg or something. I have to stay here. Ma'll be home at dinner-time and everything's got to be ready."

Then I remembered: "No," I said, "I can't! I'm going fishin' this mornin' with Jimmy and Roly Brophy ... Auntie Kate said I could!"

But, she said: "Sorry Billy, but I'm going to have to ask you to give it a miss today. Pleeease ... ?? Don't let me down on this one!"

What could I say? I was always a sucker for a line like that, especially when it came from Anna.

But what was I going to tell the lads? Not the truth anyway: Searching for Agnes! Told to by Anna! I'd never live it down.

That was what concerned me on leaving the house, not any fate that might have befallen Agnes, and I hadn't even started blaming her yet for causing me to miss my fishing trip.

The park that Anna was talking about was a good step from where we lived, but it was the nearest thing to an earthly paradise that we knew of. For the very young, there were swings, see-saws and roundabouts, and then, when you got a bit older, there were grassy banks that you could wear the arse out of your trousers sliding down, and a forest where you could hide and jump out on your mate from, when they passed you by. And there were the posh kids, who played tennis behind the meshed fences, whom you could laugh and shout at: "Mind you don't strain yourself there, Nigel!" And, if you got older still, there was even a neglected bandstand, where you could get drunk and take drugs in.

I'd never gone there after dark though, and I doubted if Agnes would have had the nerve to either, supposing that that was where Herbert went, and who ever said that it was?

* * *

As it was still not long past eight o' clock, and as I wasn't due at Conroy's until nine, I came up with the clever, but, admittedly, spineless scheme of a scribbled note pushed quietly through their letterbox, as my easiest way out. But I was caught!

I'd slipped over their front wall, tip-toed up the garden path and was poised to deliver, when the door suddenly opened, and Jimmy's father, oblivious, it seemed, to what I held over him, said: "Fair dues to ye, Billy Boy, up with the lark! C'mon in an' I'll shift him for ye!"

I, letting him up the stairs, tore up the note, and threw it with it's lie – something about having to go somewhere with Herbert – into the unlit fireplace, and waited. I sat down shivering. It was cold. I was tired. Jimmy's father didn't reappear.

There was a commotion upstairs: Jimmy's father shouted at Jimmy; then Mickey shouted at him; then Jimmy shouted at him too; then Mickey shouted at Jimmy; then the echos of a scuffle; then more oaths and death-threats, until I heard Patrick asking everyone to: "Calm down please!" Then nothing - all sound and motion ceased. What to do now? I'd made a balls of it!

I couldn't retrieve the note and leave it for Jimmy: in my panic, I'd torn it to shreds. But it didn't matter now anyway, because he must have been told that I was downstairs. I couldn't take the chance of him getting up, especially on my account, and my not being there. And I certainly wasn't going to go up and disturb him! So, resolutely, I picked up a bike magazine and looked through it, until Roly arrived at ten to nine. Ten to nine? I couldn't believe it; it still should have not been much later than, just gone eight o'clock!

Not long before, I'd lain awake watching the hands of a luminous alarm clock, and wondering about exactly the same thing. It certainly didn't happen when I was at school or at mass, but when I had the be up early that morning, or, I was going to be doing something that I might enjoy, or, as now, when I was trying to figure out what to do next, time jumped forward and took away any bit of leisure that I might have had. I'd felt hard done by, and decided that I must be owed.

I thought about how much I might be owed, and how I could be paid back. Maybe, it would be added on at the end? But that would be no use, because how would I know the difference? If I lived to be eighty, how could I be certain that if it wasn't for time paying me back , I wouldn't have got past sixty-three, or, maybe, seventy two? No, the only way I could envisage me getting my dues was, say, to be walking down the street, and a voice to boom, periodically, from the Heavens, something like: "Okay Billy Sikes, I see that I owe you eight days, eleven hours, seventeen minutes and six seconds, so off you go now, and never let it be said ... ," and I'd end up in the middle of last week! I got to thinking then, about what I'd do when I got there, but I didn't get beyond forecasting the football results before I fell asleep. But, maybe that's where Agnes was? Maybe, that's where Herbert went to too?

Roly was sticking his expensive watch, that his father had bought him for his confirmation, into my face now, and saying: "You stupid cunt, will you not believe anything?" But Jimmy appeared then, and said: "Ah Siko" (That's what they called me, and I was very happy about it too: No one minded saying that they hung around with someone called "Siko," at least to people who didn't know me, and it was going to look great sprayed on the walls, when I got older.)

"Ah Siko," he said, "I didn't know you were here too!" I got my spoke in quickly: "By the way," I said, "Herbert wants me to do something with him later on, so I'll be headin' back early, okay?"

Roly snorted in the way that he did; so that you couldn't really accuse him of it, but Jimmy said: "No sweat Siko! Do your own thing! Don't worry about it!" It struck me then that Jimmy mightn't have minded if I'd said that I wasn't going at all! But it was too late now, and, anyway, maybe it wasn't such a bad plan: If I got to the park by mid, or even late-afternoon, and made a point of being seen by some of the kids from our place, who were bound to be there on a Saturday, at this time of year, I could claim to Anna that I'd been there all day! Better still, I could even add that I thought it best not to return any earlier because, taking it that Agnes would surely be back by then, Kate would be wondering why I hadn't gone fishing with the boys.

Not that I wanted to lie to Anna, but, with hope now, I could leave Conroy's feeling not nearly as bad as I had been.

* * *

I liked sitting on the bus looking out at the countryside. I seemed particularly attracted to cows and fields, and trees with no kids around them, probably because I hadn't been on that many trips yet. I wasn't a veteran like Jimmy, who could, ignoring it all, smoke his cigarette and tell more tales of Mickey.

Roly didn't smoke, because he was to mean to, but myself and Jimmy chipped in for ten, whenever we went now. In the beginning I felt sick, but that was really only for the first couple, after that I was able to enjoy them. And I wasn't addicted: I didn't have to assault old ladies handbags, or sell my body to strangers (Whatever it was they might want it for?) to finance my habit, like the addicts they talked about on television.

They told us in school all about the dangers of smoking. In fact, the teacher who did most of the telling smoked himself, but when Jimmy pointed this out to him, he hit him with his cane and made him turn out his pockets. They told us of how cigarettes would stop us growing, and make our lungs turn brown. They even showed us a film that featured an old man struggling to climb up a flight of stairs.

He wasn't much of a film star, I'll have to admit! He was wrinkled and decrepit, and had bits of dinner down his tie and jacket; either that or they were pieces of lung tissue that he'd coughed up. He couldn't even close his fly properly – somebody noticed. When he'd make it up a couple of steps, he'd stop gasping and holding his hand to his chest.

I waited for a stain to appear on his trousers; I couldn't see why else he'd be so desperate to get up there! I reckoned, if it was me, and I was in a condition like he was, I'd just pee out in the back garden. Unless there was a girl up there, waiting for him? There could well have been, if he'd been a character in another film; one that wasn't about smoking. But, maybe that's what they told him? And him being senile, although still aware enough to know that he might never get that kind of opportunity again, had fallen for it.

I could see it: Some flashy, executive-producer type of anti-enjoyment films for primary schools bastard in a shiny suit, and with a cigar in his mouth too, scouring the super-geriatric wards of old folks hospitals ,with his sneaky looking sidekicks, for ninety-eight year old imbeciles dying from horrendous lung diseases that were, in reality, not caused by smoking at all, but by the foul chemicals that were fed to them through the air-conditioning apparatus near their beds, to star in his films. They were probably brought out and made run first! I couldn't bring myself then, to clap along with everyone else, when our man, having finally made it to the landing, collapsed and died?

Anyway, didn't it just go to show that even smokers could get to be very old! Not that I was bothered either way; I didn't want to get beyond thirty – even younger, before Herbert –

what would I do then? I'd be fit for nothing except, maybe, having kids and a wife who told me what to do, until she got fed up and went off with someone else. Neither did I care if I didn't grow much more, people were already saying that I was getting to be a right "lanky little bastard." And if my lungs turned brown, who'd notice? No one was going to turn me inside out! Unlike nicotine stains on your fingers, and they weren't even a problem, once you took a 'Brillo' pad to them every now and again. The way it was then, anyone who was anybody smoked. That's why people like Roly Brophy didn't!

I blew some of it now in his direction and he gave me one of his filthier looks, and said: "How's that mad brother of yours?" Jimmy had to hold me back! If someone else had said it, it could have been meant as a compliment: "Mad" could have been "Mad" as in "Mad" Mickey Conroy, or "Mad" as in someone who fought and drank all the time. But that was definitely not the way that Roly meant it.

If we ever did come to blows though, and we often nearly did, I think that he would have won. And not just because he was bigger and thicker than I was, but because of his rotten disposition. Roly couldn't have fought cleanly; he couldn't just have punched you, or kicked you, in the face like anyone else; he would have had to scrab you with his fingernails, and then send his mother up to you the next day. It was just as well that Jimmy was always there!

Roly hated me going on the trips, and the worst for him must have been when Jimmy made him lend me his fishing rod. I intended, someday, to get one of my own, but as yet I hadn't even got, as Roly pointed out, as much as "a decent maggot," and he, maybe needless to say, had all the gear.

But I was happy enough just to sit there looking out over the lake, until Jimmy would ask me to: "Catch us a few Siko," and hand me his. Although, I never did, because at the slightest hint of a bite, he'd insist on giving me a "dig out." Then, after a while, he'd take it back, and say:"Let him in there now Roly." Roly would mumble, so that we couldn't hear a word of what he said, although we could understand what he meant alright, and Jimmy would say: "What?" and he'd say:"Nothing!" and give up his rod with another one of his looks, and spit, so that I'd spit too, but further – I was a good spitter; a lousy whistler, but a good spitter – and then Roly would spit again, and then so would I, and then ... and then Jimmy would outspit both of us, and that would be the end of it. That happened at least once!

On this particular day though, there was no one smoking, nor was there anyone spitting. We were all just sitting there; the boys fishing, and me looking out over the lake, when I saw him: The Fish King.

* * *

There was someone talking though: It was Jimmy. We hadn't long arrived, in fact, we'd only just found ourselves an agreeable spot, not that there was a lot of people there, there wasn't; the lakeside was deserted, but because of Roly's being awkward again, which, though, really didn't count for anything, me having the deciding vote.

There was never much competition for spaces beside the lake, not even on a Saturday morning. On my first visit there, we ran off when a man had shouted at us from a boat, but Jimmy had explained to me afterwards, that it wasn't that fishing wasn't allowed, it was just that you weren't supposed to keep what you caught. At least, you could do on to the perch what you liked, but the trout were meant to go back in. It occurred to me then, whilst impaling some more worms on Jimmy's hooks, that there must be a lot of fat, battled-scarred creatures swimming around out there.

Not that we put our trout back in; mostly we sold them in the pub on the way home, or Jimmy did, and even shared out the proceeds. But it couldn't have been that risky anyway, or Roly wouldn't have been doing it.

The worst part of fishing for me though, was when someone actually caught one, and then swung it by the tail and bashed it's brains out on a rock. I mean, I loved being there, but that bothered me. And it wasn't that I was any kind of "Save the Fish" freak, or that I wanted to put them in a bowl and call them names. I suppose, other than when they were having their heads smashed open, I couldn't have cared less about them. No, what I think it was, was that it reminded me of a trick that Agnes had played on me when I was younger. I could never forget it!

She'd put chocolate in a mousetrap, and then had stood there laughing when I nearly lost my fingers. But by the time that Kate got home, she'd restocked it with cheese and taken it out of my cot, so that I got into trouble for poking into places where I shouldn't. I identified with those battered fish.

But Jimmy and Roly were keeping them away now by arguing the capabilities of Mickey's new bike or, at least, the one he aspired to.

"I'm tellin' you," Jimmy said, "It'll do at least ninety-five, he had it on the road up there, and it was touchin' the ton on the clock!"

"No way," Roly disagreed, "there's not a one-two-five that's been made yet that'll go that fast."

"This one will," Jimmy said, "You can ask Mickey! Even ask any of his mates; they'll tell you!"

"I don't need to ask anyone," Roly countered, " I know! There's not a hope in ... "

Jimmy had run into trouble here: It was generally accepted that when it came to technical specifications and the like, Roly was a way ahead of his class. Even when he was in Conroy's and picked up a magazine, he didn't just look at the pictures and read the bits that everyone else did, but studied the graphs and figures on the pages that were supposed to be skipped. And he had no intention of conceding on this one.

If it had been me, and Jimmy had said that the bike that Mickey had at the moment, the little one, did one hundred and fifty miles an hour and had a reverse gear, I would just have said: "Is that right, Jimmy!"

But Roly could get very stroppy about things like that, and even though Jimmy knew it too, he just couldn't help himself. If Jimmy, for any reason, ever went to Japan and happened to bump into Mister Honda himself, I reckoned that he'd try to convince even him, that Mickey's bikes went faster than they really did. And it wasn't that Jimmy was dishonest, far from it! He was just inclined to be a bit of a dreamer sometimes – that was all.

Roly hadn't any brothers, but his father, it seemed, was a lot like himself, and he tried to bring him in whenever he could:"Well you're wrong there," he'd say, "because my Da says ... and he's an engineer." And that might be just when you were discussing the likelihood of it raining or not. It was only years later that I discovered that he didn't drive a train!

Jimmy, sensing Roly's father coming though, warded him off. Always resourceful, he had a talent for tackling a situation like this one. He cast out his line: "Soon as he gets it," he said,"he's gonna give me his old one."

And Roly took the bait: "You're havin' me on!" he said. But you could tell by the way that his piggy little eyes opened wide that he didn't mean it. Roly's mind was so cluttered with graphs and figures that he was always going to be flummoxed by someone with Jimmy's imagination.

I didn't believe it. It was outrageous! Everyone knew that after women, Jimmy's father probably hated motorcycles next. Hadn't he seen his own brother being "scraped o' the tarmac" back in Scotland, after he'd been let down by one! And big and all as Mickey was, he still told him to, "git that fuckin' death machine away from my doer," when he had the humour. Although, of course Mickey didn't, but still and all, if he did what Jimmy had said he was going to do, it was just possible that he'd have to be peeled of the gravel too. Anyway, Jimmy was a long way from being old enough, and his father didn't like policemen around his "doer" either.

But Jimmy was away with it now; revealing his plans on inheriting his legacy. I'd been party to them before, but in the earlier editions they weren't to become tangible for another couple of years yet.

So it was, that we were heading west , the three of us, me on the pillion, with Roly and the gear piled in the sidecar beside us – "It'll pull anything!" Jimmy had said – when an unseen hand pitched a large stone into the middle of the lake, and from the formation of the outmost of the resultant ripples appeared the rear ends of a spectacular shoal of small fish, who, promptly, spun heads over tails, and with their little fishy mouths opening wide, like mine must have been, sang:

"Here comes the King, here comes the King,
we've gathered around to make up his ring."

The centre of their circle then became a bubbling cauldron, and from it's depths emerged the kind of scaly monster that would have done credit to another lake: Ness.

But if he was a monster he was indeed a regal one, for atop his glistening pate he wore a crown, shining threw the smoke that rose from the fat cigar clenched between his, hook-marked, smirking jowls. Then, slowly, surfacing further, he revealed the royal charger, a mount favoured by that other incredible fish: Jimmy's red herring; a Honda C50.

* * *

I couldn't say how the others were reacting, because I was transfixed to the scene. My head, not even my eyes, would move, and when I tried to shout: "Oh shit!", the best my voice could do was to whisper it. The circle opened then and transformed itself into two opposing ranks, and the King, taking their salute, rode out, with his entourage now in tow – directly over to me!

Unwrapping some fish fingers from the bars (I supposed, he had to hold on somehow!), he withdrew his cigar, exhaled a cloud of smoke – It was a very big cigar – and said: "Hop on kid, we're going for a ride!"

So there I was, on a Saturday morning, by the side of a lake, being summoned aboard by a crown-wearing, cigar-smoking, man-sided, motorcycling trout who was now patting his pillion with his slippery tail. And I'd been afraid that nothing exciting was ever going to happen in my life! Of course, I obliged!

Comfortably unaware of either my backside soaking, or my stomach retching from the stench of his slimy scales, we rode back to the centre of the lake, where the fish again surrounded, but this time with a different fanfare:

"Now the fish that you seek have themselves a man (In the widest possible sense, I assumed!) to keep."

And the King, in a manner reminiscent of that earlier demonstrated by his subjects, revving the throttle, flipped up his front wheel and toppled us backwards into the dusky waters.

Now as an avid viewer of 'Voyage to the Bottom of the Sea,' I might have expected to know what came next. Many's the hour, the ladies' permitting, or, better still, marked absent, I'd spent with the crew down there, marvelling at the exotic magnificence of the underwater flora and fauna that could thrive even on our black and white TV. Often too, I'd shivered when confronted with the evil intentions of, multi-tentacled, octopussy things who'd sought to squeeze the life out of us, or our machine. And I'd been shaken, with the rest of them, by the terrible weaponry of other deposed humankinds, who resented our intrusion into their, nefarious, sub-aquatic activities.

But in the King's company, I was exposed to neither beauty or peril, just to a rushing of water that made me deaf and then blind, until a light appeared in the darkness.

* * *

I still didn't know where the light was coming from, when the King, invisible in the downsurge, made another royal appearance, and surprised me further by looking less the mutated trout now, and more the common or garden motorcyclist in a, helmeted, wax-jacketed, gloved and booted sort of way. Neither then, was the road we travelled akin to a causeway of Neptune, but no more waterlogged than one that had been subject to a light drizzle in the recent past. And if the neatly-trimmed lawns around the semi and detached houses we passed were unnatural, they were no more so than those adjoining the park, where I really should have been that day.

The King then, not at all resplendent in the bright sunshine, and again in the manner of the common masses, obeying most of the rules of the road, guided his machine through a flow of average suburban traffic (There may have been something peculiar about it, but I wasn't sure what. More rounded lines, perhaps?) until, with the appropriate hand signals, he divided a pair of low-cropped hedges and steered us up a driveway to the door of a garage, that swivelled miraculously, so that we entered, and he, turning off the engine, could say to me, in barely intelligible English: "Well, here we are son!"

Barely intelligible English, because I too had sprouted some headgear making conversation all the more difficult. We dismounted, and I removed the crash helmet, and the balaclava beneath it too, and followed him into the house, where he, with all but his gloves still in place (He had man's hands now, but fishy-eyed yet?), said: "Back in a tic." So, not knowing how long 'a tic' was, and knackered as I again felt, I pulled out a chair from beneath a table and settled myself down. I was in a kitchen! But one that was, with it's strange apparatus and remarkable spaciousness, unlike Kate's, or anyone else's that I'd ever visited.

The 'tic' didn't last long, because I'd only become interested in the procession of grim-faced, soberly-clothed, legless men who glided past the window, when he said: "Saturday dog walk!"

"Personally, I prefer bigger ones," I said.

"Yes," he agreed " but the small ones are easier to keep."

Apart from the balaclava, that he still had on, the King had undergone another remarkable transformation: his jacket and boots having been replaced with a polo-neck sweater and slippers, matching in darkness the trousers that he wore. Sitting across from me then, he said: "What age are you son?" And, I answering: "Eleven and three-quarters," was immediately mortified.

I couldn't believe what I'd just said! I hadn't claimed to have been anything and three-quarters, since I was about eight and three quarters! Quarters were the stuff of kids and schoolteachers. Teachers were forever on about quarters, and thirds and eights as well - but that was school! Outside of it, the only quarters you needed to know about were quarters of bull's-eyes, maybe, not that you'd be buying them yourself, but someone else might be, or, "it's quarter to ... ," when there was something good on the television at eight. Or, maybe, showing the enemy "no quarter lads," in an old battle, perhaps, but, otherwise you had no use for them.

Halves were enough, especially when you had "big halves" and "little halves," as in: "I bags the big half," of an apple or a piece of chewing gum, or anything else that you were dividing evenly. And then there was half-time in football matches, that you, when you weren't playing, looked forward to in the hope that you might get a game, or, if you were playing, dreaded, because you knew you were going to be taken off. There was even "half-term" in the books that Anna read, and "half rations" in the war picture ones, that Jimmy had given me.

Outside of school, quarters were only for the likes of Roly Brophy who, if you mentioned it to him, would probably argue that, in actuality, I wasn't eleven and three quarters, at all, but only eleven and nine-sixteenths, or something like that.

Maybe I was in shock? People were said to do and say things when they were "in shock" that were completely out of character. But then, that was only if they were popular; if they weren't, nobody would have expected anything better from them, anyway. Baddies would always be acting in character, and be baddies, no matter what film they were in.

"A good age," he said, "you've time yet."

"For what?" I asked.

But,"Are you hungry?" he replied. "I mean … will you eat? I can do you something up in a jiffy!"

"No thanks," said I. In a jiffy or on a plate I didn't want anything. I hadn't thought about food at all that day, and I wasn't about to start now. And, anyway, I'd been warned, although I don't know by who, about not taking sweets, or anything else, I presumed, from strange men, and they couldn't come much stranger than this man/fish now smiling at me, through his black mask, from across the table.

"How about a Coke?" he said.

That was different!

We didn't have a fridge at home, but I was happy that I'd know what to look for, but the tall, chesty thing that he went to bore little resemblance to my idea of one. If I'd have known him better, I might have come out with something really witty, like: "What do you keep in there … bodies?"

Reading my mind though, he explained: "We don't shop very often … stock up," and pulling open a drawer, he withdrew a bottle, unscrewed the cap, placed it in front of me and said: "Drink up!"

I thanked the good Lord that I didn't, or, at least, not in one go, that I'd attempted some show of politeness by not lashing it back, but had merely slugged a good mouthful, but still he saw me squirming.

"Oh sorry!" he apologised, "it's an irregular blend: sugar free and with all of the additives taken out. You're probably…you're probably used to …" he paused again …"the real thing!"

"But," he said, "we've got orange juice as well, if you'd like to try some of that?"

I declined, but not wanting to completely rebuke his hospitality, said: "A glass of water would be fine thanks."

"Water," he smiled again, "is no problem at all!"

If nothing else, thought I, I'd landed in the house of a gentleman. That's if that title was appropriate for one of such changeable species, who was now acting extraordinarily again by seeking not a tap, but returning to the fridge, where from, he produced another bottle, saying: "The mains stuff is contaminated, full of harmful pollutants, this won't taste like what you're used to either, but it's not so bad, really."

Smiling politely back at him, I'd already decided to take his word for it, when it succeeded the Coke, he making that all the easier by not immediately retaking his seat but, once more, behaving in a manner that I wouldn't have previously equated with reality: Speechlessly, he paced up and down, with his head thrust forward, and his hands clasped behind his back, until, eventually, he did sit down, and said:"What follows isn't suitable for younger viewers."

Well okay, he didn't! He said: "You're only a slip of a lad and you might find some of this a bit difficult, but you're here so I'll tell you."

I was enthralled, of course!

I could consider myself experienced in this kind of situation: hadn't I been convulsed by fits of laughter in mass, blown-off when the headmaster was visiting our classroom and had thrown-up on the only coach trip I was ever allowed to go on. But I didn't feel any less awkward when, for fear of the consequences of not doing so, I said to him, before he'd gotten started: "Can I use your toilet please?" I even put my hand up, as far as I recall.

He took it well though, even if he looked as if he'd had to think about it first.

"Certainly," he said then, "no problem ... It's at the top of the stairs ... I'll show you!"

Leading me to the doorway, he'd recently entered, he said, pointing: "Straight up ... you can't miss it! Take it easy though," he warned, "the wife's asleep."

It was easy to take it easy: I'd never trodden on a thicker carpet before, and it carried me all the way to the bathroom, where confused again by an array of unfamiliar conveniences, I made, I realised, if only later in life, my first, hasty acquaintance with a showering unit. Re-buttoning my fly then, blissfully unaware of my error, I stooped to examine another curiosity.

It was after this inspection of what I could only imagine to be; some type of peculiarly designed drinking fountain, that, unbending, I backed into an overcrowded shelf of toiletries and sent the excess splattering downwards, to rebound, thoughtlessly, noisily, of, amongst other things, the aforementioned piece. Recoiling in horror, I was responsible for even more damage, and paid for my awkwardness when, from the depths of it's hidden chamber, a female voice boomed: "For fuck sake Joseph! Will you keep it fuckin' down; I can't get a bloody wink!"

Protecting my identity, although with no harm intended to Joseph (For that must be the man/fish's name!), I shakily, but as quietly as possible, refitted the bits and pieces on the shelf as best as I could, and descended warily, passing Joseph on the way, who was, I could hear, already whispering his apologies.

He followed me down then, and said: "Don't worry about it son, it wasn't your fault; that bathroom's full of trash, it's next to impossible to move without disturbing something, particularly the wife, and it doesn't take a lot to disturb her.

Although," he said, "It's the same with all women, I suppose?"

"I know," I agreed, "I live (Lived?) with a houseful of them, even the dog was a bitch!" (That was true; we'd once had a psychotic terrier who'd claimed to belong to Agnes.)

"Maybe," he said, "that's why I've got to talk to you."

* * *

He'd been in his twenties, he told me, and working on a building site, but not all of the time; in the evenings he'd played with a band: "Myself and a couple of lad's I'd known," he said, "and the man who had got us together; he who named us: "The Loveliest People in the Land of Mary."

"At first," he said, "we played cover versions of rock classics in bars around town. I knew we weren't very good but, somehow, he was always able to arrange somewhere for us, so much so, that we were moving around a lot, and playing, maybe, three or four nights a week. We gotten to be quite popular, and were making a bit of money, as well. But then, he decided that we should start to do our own stuff, that's when the problems began."

"Now, it's not that we weren't ambitious," he said, "We didn't speak about it, but I think we were all quietly dreaming of a bit of fortune and fame – I know I was! And we'd had enough of performing the old tunes. It had even been said to us that, because we were known now, there were agents from the record companies who, if we did anything half-decent, at all, were just waiting to sign us up. But he wasn't having it!"

"He insisted that we should only create the music that we ourselves wanted to hear: that we should go on stage and play just whatever it was that came to hand; to deny anything that was contrived or repeated. We were, he told us, to declare war on 'The smiling guitarist,' the, 'I shot the sheriff ... yes I did ... yes I did' merchant, who trotted out tired old arrangements, whilst trying to let everyone know that he was aware of it, in a smiling attempt at self-justification."

"And lyrics were out of the question too, unless they were completely spontaneous: he saying that, 'the best poetry having never been written,' which, all in all, wasn't much use to the record producers, excepting that they wanted to come along and record one of our live shows, but that's only if they were able to get in! That was the really peculiar part of it all; we were never more popular, I think we'd become some sort of cult band. Personally, I was amazed at he amount of people who'd pay to have us stand in front of them, twanging purposelessly on our instruments, more times than not, totally out of accord with each other."

"We weren't happy though! I argued that it must be wrong for us to be so self-indulgent; that surely we had some sort of responsibility to try and stretch ourselves, to relate to and entertain others, apart from the odd-balls who attended our shows. But, he said, no; that our only responsibility was to ourselves, and that if we consciously tried to connect with a wider audience, it could only be for some sort of personal gain, it would involve a compromise, and any connection we might make then would be, merely, a superficial one. If people did, or didn't, attend when we were doing our stuff, that was all well and good, but we couldn't dilute it, or polish it up for anyone, and if that meant that we were never going to make any great worldly gains, then, so be it! We always had to do, only what we felt was right."

"I argued that what 'we' felt, was actually what 'he' felt, and as far as 'I' was concerned, what we were doing was rubbish. But, he said, that by joining up with any sort of band, we sacrificed the greater part of the 'I', that we, automatically, seconded our individual priorities to those of the combined unit, and so interlinked it with our destinies, regardless of who, or what, it was that tried to shape them. But, he reminded me that I was, and always would be, free to leave."

"Why didn't you," I asked, "go and join another band?"

"Well," he said, "I didn't fancy starting from scratch and probably ending up as bad, or, maybe, worse off; at least we had a following. And I did believe in him! It seemed unlikely, but there was always the chance that we would create something magical."

"Anyway," he said, "I owed him everything: I couldn't even play an instrument when we started – he taught me how to learn!"

"I suppose," he said, "it was a case of 'The Devil you know.'"

"Did you always want to be in a band?" I asked.

"No," he replied, "I never expected to get more involved in music than to listen to it. But I wanted to do something with my life; I was terrified of wasting it. So when he asked me, I said: 'Why not!'

"But that was the kind of man that he was: If he asked you to do anything, you'd be inclined to say, 'Why not!' He had a way with him; a power. And he'd appeared from nowhere, no one knew anything about him; he'd just appeared on our streets in the evenings, with his hat and his brown paper-bag, looking like Frank Zappa – a lot of people had said."

"So did you," I asked, "hit upon your masterwork?"

"I don't think so ... well not in my time anyway," he said, "because along came 'The Green Eyes!'"

* * *

I hadn't noticed the brown paper-bag, but then I'd never really got a good look at him, when he was heading out of an evening. But it could explain why Agnes had made quacking sounds and called "Fucky Ducky" after him, on more than one occasion. I'd assumed that she was accusing him of being a homosexual, everyone knowing that homosexuals called each other "Ducky" in those days. Which was bad enough, but if I'd have thought that she was suggesting that he was, somehow, because I couldn't picture it, I couldn't even try to, having sexual relations with a duck, I would have ... well I don't know what I would have done! But, anyway, whatever was in the bag that Herbert carried with him, was sure to be something much more meaningful than a few breadcrumbs to court a duck with.

Joseph was on stage again: "So there we were," he said, "playing away, it was to be one of our last gigs before we went abroad."

"Abroad?" I said

"Yes," he said, "he told us that if we wanted to widen our audience we'd have to spread ourselves around, and the story of 'The Mountain and Muhammed': If the mountain can't come to Muhammed, then Muhammed must go to the mountain. And, so it was, that we were heading for the hills of Holland; it was all arranged. And, anyway, I was looking forward to it; I'd always wanted to travel a bit, and had thought that I might never get the opportunity. But then when I was looking for him, looking at us (He didn't play himself.), I saw them: 'The Green Eyes!'"

"They were tucked in next to, but didn't belong to, a group of know-it-all, phoney idealists, whom we'd always tried to avoid when they arrived in for a late joint, and they were fixed right upon me!"

"I was entranced! I kept thumping away on my bass, but otherwise I was frozen, and when we'd finished, I couldn't but go down and buy the woman they belonged to a drink. Her name was Marian, and we had a second one."

"That was it," he said, "I never got away! I couldn't have left her, even without her trying to convince me that I'd be crazy to pack in my job, although she did suggest that I should go to college in the evenings and study for a better one – me being but a humble carpenter back then – I'm a programs analyst now," he said

I didn't know what a programs analyst was, but it sounded as if it was right up my street!

"In the beginning," he went on, "I'd no regrets about not going away, we were having a great time. We went out and got drunk together, we stayed in and got stoned together, we watched films and read the same books, we listened to music and went off for weekends; I had a bike then too. Or, we just hung around her flat, even before I'd moved in. Best of all for me though, was being able to talk to her about all the stuff that no one else would want to listen to."

"But then," he said, "when we were still only together for a matter of months, she showed the first signs of her illness: It started with the curtains; after she'd drawn them in the evenings, she wouldn't sit down, but would stand there for ages, in front of the television too, adjusting the creases. Then it was the furniture; she'd ease it this way and that, and then hover around scrutinising her angles, and she couldn't sit for ten minutes on the couch without pumping up the cushions around us. She even got to rearranging my feet on the table where I'd left them."

"From there," he said, "she deteriorated rapidly. She threw out newspapers and magazines before I'd read them, she froze me out of it by opening windows and waving her arms about where I'd been smoking. The flat reeked of air-freshener and, when I came home in the evenings, she insisted that I left my boots on the doorstep, even though she'd lain plastic sheeting all over the hallway carpet. She even made the bed with me still in. And that was just the physical stuff," he said.

"She became possessive. At the start we'd agreed that we'd never try to own each other, but now, if I even mentioned another woman, she wouldn't speak to me for days or, worse, became aggressive. But then, she didn't want to hear most of what I said now, or, if she did, she'd take it up the wrong way; she was seriously paranoid!"

"It got that I couldn't open my mouth, even the weather was dangerous: 'A lovely day,' she construed as my sarcastic after-throw to an earlier argument, one that I had already forgotten about. And, of course, I couldn't say that I thought it was going to rain, or she'd think that I was trying to get out of doing something, that she wanted me to."

"She was convinced that I was always trying to talk down to her, or, at least, when I wasn't, I was plotting against her. If I as much as tried to give my opinion on anything, she'd contradict me, or demand to know if I thought that she wasn't able to see the same, and who the hell did I think I was anyway?"

"But she certainly needn't have worried herself about my thinking about myself as her intellectual superior," he said, "the woman was a genius! Sherlock Holmes himself would have found it impossible to construct the cases against me that she did from the flimsiest of evidence. And I was found guilty on all counts: dishonesty, infidelity, hypocrisy, slothfulness, heresy, bigotry, blasphemy ... and if I hadn't committed it yet, it was only because I was still planning it. Although, in certain circumstances, she might have accepted insanity as a plea, because she'd thrown that one at me many times when I'd tried to get through to her. I was lonely again. To be honest, my life was a misery."

He paused, so I asked: "What became of her?"

"She's upstairs in bed," he said. "That was her shouting."

We allowed a respectful silence to elapse between us, before I asked: "And the band?"

"Oh, they went off without me.," he replied, "I suppose, I was a bit disappointed that he didn't try to change my mind, but he never said a thing. I heard they broke up, though, after only a short time away: I bumped into the lead guitarist, and he told me; he having fallen for a pair of legs, and the drummer running off with an accent. And the man himself disappeared, no one knew where he went to."

"You never saw him again?" I said.

"I did," he answered, "but only in my dreams."

* * *

"It was like a video playing in my head," he said

"A what?" I asked.

"No matter," he replied, "suffice to say that I always watch the same movie or it's sequels."

"I was in a bank," he began "in a lengthy queue, it was slow-moving and I was restless. Upfront, the stuffy-looking teller in his cage would have tried the patience of a monk at the zenith of all understanding with the time he was taking over the notes and forms that were passing back and forth. I was considering leaving my business until another day, when, suddenly, for no apparent reason, as they are wont to do, the queue jumped forwards, and I was left with just a little old lady and a schoolboy ahead of me. The little old lady, though, appeared to be on conversational terms with the teller, and we were halted again while they chatted."

"It was then that the schoolboy, and I call him that only because he wore the clothing to suit, lifted his cap, revealing a small package perched on the top of his head, which he removed and placed in the old lady's shopping bag, laid on the floor beside her. He bothered me more then, by turning to show me the face of a forty year old, and, in his short trousers, leaving with the legs to match."

"Now, my first impulse was to tap the old lady on the shoulder and inform her of what had occurred, and my reasons for not doing so are still unclear; self-consciousness in an unfamiliar environment, maybe? Or, the inertia that has dogged me all my days, perhaps? I couldn't say! But what I can say, is that I told myself that it was possible, likely even, that the schoolboy was her extraordinary son, and that his action was in some way a legitimate one. I didn't want to get involved!"

"Anyway, when she'd finished her chat, I allowed her to pass, feigning the appearance of one who was scrutinising the documents in his hand for the first time, and then took up position where she'd vacated. It was only after the teller had, gruntingly, set about my affair that I felt the rub against my shin, and looked down to see the old lady's shopping bag!"

"Turning, I saw that she was still bidding her goodbyes to the security guard, who'd unlocked the door beneath the 'Baggage Check' sign, and this time, guided by a stronger impulse, I grabbed the bag and hastened across, only to have her collapse into his arms when I got there. But the guard assuring me that he would take care, I, dropping my head, flushed with embarrassment, shuffled back to where I'd been. I didn't make it!"

"Just like the fallen old lady, perhaps, I too was overtaken by an attack of the senses: My eardrums screaming with the pain of noise, and my eyes quivering red before me, I soared upwards, passing the lady burning, animated once again, her head bowing to scuttle, flaming, along the floor beneath us. The guard's arm, sprightly yet in it's uniform cuff, but similarly unattached now, bid me halt, and failing to do so, I was accosted by the stuffy teller who, lunging through his cage, but with some of the bars still pierced through him, head-butted me furiously in the groin, and then dropped to seek repentance between the legs of his lady-friend."

"I rose higher and higher, until, like the avenging angel, I returned back through the smoke and flame, and came to rest on the street outside. My wits still prey to the forces that shifted light and descended masonry, screaming people obliterating in the fusion, I lay with my head pressed into the dust, unable, or, afraid, to move, until from above me, a woman's voice, softly undamaged by the turmoil, said: "Come with me, you the chosen!"

* * *

I'd heard about the chosen people; Elijah had often spoken about them. I wondered was that why Joseph wore the mask: to hide his nose? Not that you had to be Jewish to have a bad nose, I was very aware of the fact, but I was far too polite to ask, and, anyway, I had nothing against Jews; I hadn't even known any yet!

Supposedly, there were plenty of them living around the park, where I really should have been that day, but I'd never met them. Neither, had I met any Niggers or Pakis; they only liking to live in England then, which must have been great for the white kids over there, who, otherwise, would have been picked on. Nor any Queers, that I was sure of, but still, I would have had to say that I hated them, if anyone asked.

Joseph continued: "I raised my head, I could! And through the haze, I saw her pointing, in God knows what direction. Running then, chasing after her, barely visible, across the fallen buildings and smoking bodies, we came to a jeep, stranded, waiting to pull us through the carnage of the broken day."

"A party, eight or ten strong, of white-dressed, ski-masked figures, unconcerned, it seemed, by the explosions still surrounding, blocked our passage with the menace of their waving machine-guns. But, undeterred, she stood down on the accelerator and scattered them groundwards, to punctuate the discordance after us with the whining of their bullets. Another white party appeared ahead, but, mercifully, ignored us, occupied as they were with the mowing down of fleeing pedestrians, and I, overcome by the horror of it all, withdrew, only to come to in entirely different circumstances."

"Pushing back a cross-barred gate, she, indistinct still in her, emerald-hued, combat gear, was opening the way for us to roll up a tree-scented and overhung laneway, to a thatched-roof cottage where, helping me down, she led me through to a single-bedded room, and then left so that I could rest again. It was when she returned that I, enraptured, became her slave!"

"Better to talk to you," he said "who are so young, than to one who is so old as to have forgotten."

I was to be assailed then by the kind of talk that I couldn't have hoped for for many a month yet!

* * *

"She was dark", he said, "and she was beautiful. Her cheekbones smiled, and her lips glowed like a beacon for the lost. Her eyes captivated me and buried me within her. She'd held a tray, but laid it down to undo the blouse that she was wearing. Opening it wide, she showed me her large firm breasts, cupping one then with her hand and stroking the scarlet nipple, her other hand thrust up beneath her tight, short skirt and, without taking her eyes from me, she spread her long, bronzed legs and rubbed between them, gently at first, but then vigorously. She leant against the doorway for support, her lips parted, her tongue protruding wildly, now gasping audibly."

"Afraid that I wouldn't for long more be able to control myself, I pleaded with her to come over. She did, panting, with her skirt pulled up around her waist and her high heels dangling. She lowered herself down to me. I grasped her breasts, my tongue finding a jutting nipple. Feverishly, she reached for my groin, pulling open my trousers, she ..."

Wow! Maybe, I'd have to use the bathroom again? Other than a couple of vividly remembered, but sadly dated, "I'll show you, if you'll show me" sessions with Anna, my sexual education to now had, apart from the leisurely perusal of a filthy book that I'd chanced upon beneath Agne's pillow, been restricted, mainly, to Jimmy's stories of brother Mickey's exploits, who was, it seemed, way beyond the "bit of tit" stage, and had even got more than his hand into the knickers of a remarkable proportion of the local female population. And he'd no regard for age or status either: Jimmy had had him, when still not much more than in his middle teens, as the main suitor to a certain glamorous widow, who was all of thirty-five, and had brought about the tragic demise of her loved one, due entirely, it was told locally, to the unnatural excessiveness of her, previously - Mickey had sorted her out - insatiable, sexual desires.

She too was, word had it, indiscriminate in her choice of partners, and was attracted to everything male, no matter how young or old. Kate even warning me of this, I spent nigh on a week loitering outside her house, but with not as much as a come-in. My only consolation was when she stooped about her garden chores and I, from one of my hideouts, was able to get an eye-line down her cleavage, which was, if you'd seen her, fair reward in itself! I gave up though, when Kate found out and dragged me screaming to confession, only for her to ignore the sentence of the priest and his score of "Our Fathers," and banish me beaten to my room. An ongoing punishment that was, sadly, to last longer than my vigil.

And, I mustn't have been the only male in the area who'd succumbed to the same threat or discipline, because my lack of success, if that's what it was, wasn't due to the obvious competition of any rival: I'd never been sure of another's presence there, not even Mickey's! But the fact that their women, on frequent occasions, congregated in prayer outside her house, might, indeed, have kept many men away. Personally, I hid in a hedge.

The prayers of the faithful were unusual, though, in that along with the normal entreaties for bread and salvation, they were interspersed with pleas for "the brazen bitch to get the fuck out of there" or, for "the shameless hoar to take herself and her brats back to where they came from." And where that was was anyone's guess; every man standing implicated. They'd even put their petitions in writing, on the front of her house, but still she wouldn't move. Until the brats in question, aged six and five, took to coming home bruised and screaming.

Anyway, she hadn't been that good-looking, Kate had said: "Who the hell did she think she was, swanning around, nearly naked, in those bits of clothes that she wore, flaunting herself to all and sundry. If you were to scrape half that paint of her face, no man would look at her. And thirty-five? Don't make me laugh, the only time she saw that now was on the back of a bus!"

But I was really quite relieved that she'd found the strength to resist me; if she'd given me the chance, I wasn't sure that I'd have known what to do with it. I'd never even come close to "a bit of tit". The nearest I'd come, were Agnes's through the keyhole (Anna was a late developer, although she was showing signs of a budding talent!). Or, those that people boasted about in school; who'd gotten to see a foreign film. Or, the black one's, that you were allowed to see in the geographical programmes, because they didn't count.

I could claim that I had often had my hand in a girl's knickers but, unfortunately, there was never a girl attached, and it was usually at the behest of Kate, who sent me to and from the clothesline with them. I'd kept a pair of Anna's, little frilly one's too, for a while, unwashed they were, as well, but I don't like to talk about that! If I was to come across a pair with a real live girl in them though, I don't know what I'd do.

I mean how did you "screw" a girl, the way that Mickey did with so many? The thing I had, didn't look as if it was made for it, and I was reluctant to check out anyone else's. What would Jimmy think if he caught me peeking? And, although I has seen his, it was without meaning to: Jimmy could piss with no hands; he could stand there scratching his head and rooting in his back pocket, or be slowly lighting a cigarette. Or, he could pretend to be riding a motorbike, or to be having a boxing match with someone. But, other than his being a lot bigger than mine was, I couldn't spot any difference!

Actually, I'd seen Mickey's as well, and, although it was larger still, it looked just as smooth, not that I'd tried to examine it;

it was just that he was really open like that: If I was with Jimmy, and he stopped us in the street, Mickey might just lash it out there and then. But in a different way than a pervert like Cocky O' Cleary would have done; Mickey, when he was having a piss, always got us to gather around him. Another time, when I was in Conroy's, he arrived down the stairs without a stitch on him, and stood there in front of us all polishing his boots of shiny leather. Roly was a corner pisser, like myself, so I'd never been able to get a good look at his.

I was back then with Joseph for a "magnificient," and an "ecstatic," and to have his "brain explode," and right up between her legs by the sound of it, which left me even more confused! But he'd managed, it seemed, to hang on to enough of it for him to find out that her name was Mary, and that her mission was to spread peace and love among the dispossessed and the disenchanted. And there were plenty of those about during wartime.

"Oh yeah?" I said.

"Oh yeah!" he answered.

* * *

"It wasn't the kind of war that you might have heard tell of, or learnt about, in school," he said. "You do learn about wars in school?"

"Not so much in school", I replied, "as in the comics. Captain Hurricane and the rest of them are forever beating the shit out of the Krauts and the Nips."

"Okay," he said, "well it wasn't like that ... not really! There was more to it than people in different uniforms kicking the crap out of each other, although there was plenty of that going on too. It was more like as if a deadly virus had swept over the land, and communities, quiet before to be unspoken of, erupted into sudden violence."

"The bombs came from the ground as well as the air, carried in the schoolbags of children, or hidden with old ladies' shopping(!). Assistants gelignited customers in their shops, bar staff left devices under their counters, dentists gassing their patients, doctors tried poison on theirs. Child-minding mothers sub-machine gunned their fellows in the supermarkets, house-holding men climbed roofs to snipe at their neighbours. Marauding gangs engaged in pitched battles on the streets, unaware of any causes or flags, or, if they were, unsure of who they belonged to. Allegiances were changed; black became white, and then black again, no one knew who the enemy really was. Factions commandeered planes and tanks. Suicidal pilots dive-bombed barricaded houses, heavy metal crushing all resistance. There was no escape ... killing was the thing!"

"Why?" I asked.

"Because,"he said, "the Devil held sway and had unleashed his forces on the land. His fascist minions were having their day."

"What's a fascist?" I asked.

"Captain Hurricane," he replied.

We paused again, until he said: "It was in to this terrible arena that Mary went to work. Everyday she travelled to the towns and cities, where the fighting raged fiercest, to rescue more stragglers, and bringing them home, she would, as she had done for me, offer her love to them."

"You mean ... ?" I said.

"Yes," he said, "young or old, black or white, male or female, she brought them to her bed. But, unlike me, they weren't to stay, because for me she had, she told me, a special purpose. But first, I was to be her protector."

"Sometimes she'd have difficulty," he explained, "and it wasn't so much with the men as with the women: if she stumbled across a functioning couple she was loath to split it, believing, as she did, in the sanctity of such a union, no matter how transient; she liked to cart it home intact, but often when she'd set about the male part, the female, if that was the other component, would take exception. I'd be next door listening to my music, but I always kept an ear free for hers, and, many's the time, I had to rush in to help her out, maybe I'd have to hold a girl down while she ... well whatever it was that was required! Otherwise, I'd little to deal with in the way of trouble, and, at that, it was rarely serious."

"When she'd finished with them, those who chose to returned to their wars, while the rest, the greater number, gladly travelled with us to her special place: her 'Hill of Redemption,' where they could be with each other forever in peace."

"But did it not ..." I asked "did it not bother you her being ... you know ... with all those others?"(Without my consent, I have to say, I had already been exposed to a lot of, girly, love stories.)

"No," he said, "it didn't bother me; I cared for her too much to seek possession, just to be with her when I could was enough for me. What concern of mine was what she did when I couldn't be? As long as she didn't get damaged or hurt, that is."

"But then," he said, "there came a change, signalled by the procession of country-folk she was taking in. Many was the farmer, and his wife, who knew her charms. (The goats outside her door, though, were certainly only there in the capacity of someone's pets!) The fighting, concentrated before in the cities, was finding out the rural crannies. I too became familiar with the hum-drum of the everyday bombings, and she becoming pregnant, we set off to seek a safer place."

* * *

"We hadn't had any interest in accumulating money and she saying that the house couldn't be sold, the jeep being blast-damaged, we swopped it for an old motorcycle and sidecar combination and headed off. The road we travelled was a perilous one – many times we cheated death, miraculously eluding the warring bands intent on eliminating everything in their paths. Seeking sanctuary beyond the war-zone, a darkness after the lights of battle, we finally found ourselves a city to live in."

"Undisturbed it was, but sore and weary was I when we arrived: the old bike had struggled on the journey, so much so, that I'd had to, for the last stage, push along beside it. Mary, only against the sternest of her protests, remaining in the sidecar. Accommodation prices extortionate, we found shelter by a canal, beneath a disused railway bridge, where we were not to be alone, having entered into the company of some who wouldn't aspire to the life above. These drooling idiots; these fools possessing nothing but the wealth of their souls; these wise men chanting there toothless mantras; these decrepit old hags languishing in their steaming excrement, laughed at life and made us their friends."

"But we were cold, and we were hungry, and a child was due, so Mary went to work again, but now to trade her favours for whatever it was that was wanted. I tried to aid her by acting as a go-between, but with no real need: at just the merest glimpse of her, the grocer gave freely of his stock; the draper of his wares; the cobbler of his shoes; the publication his booze; the dealer his drugs; the novice her habit; the priest his vows; the schoolmistress her cane; the farmer his ass; the poet his head; the prostitute her pitch; the lawman his badge; the judge his honour; the landlord his rooms, but we weren't allowed to stay in them – not ever!"

"Not even Mary, could root out the prejudice the propertied held against the bridge-people. Not even she, could warm their hearts to those poor creatures who would have shared our comforts, as she'd insisted that they should do. And she tried and tried again, but when she'd exhausted a score or more, she conceded that the money-takers were set in stone and, her being a long time pregnant, that we'd have to think again; it was freezing beneath that bridge in the wintertime. But the fates were with us once again, and receiving word of a home derelict, we and our company moved in."

"Although, taking an upstairs room to ourselves, we were rarely on our own, being visited frequently by our friends, who brought with them gifts that they'd acquired of clothing and toys for the child. Many's the night, they'd spent with us drinking wine, shooting up heroin, or just copulating doggedly with Mary, who was now really only comfortable doing it that way. But the night our world exploded, we were alone."

"Rushing to the boarded window, we could see through the jagged gaps the sky above us ablaze, dazzling us sickening yellow. The aged walls crumbling, reverberating to a dreadful beat. The war had found us! We turned to flee, but to be swallowed whole by the floor's collapsing."

"Mindful not of physical pain, I pushed away the fallen blocks and pulled myself clear, to kneel and eye, pitifully, the empty desolation. But then, I heard her moan and moan again, and her arm, bleeding, protruded from the rubble beside me. With fist clenched, she screamed, the pile cascading, and there with her was the child – the silent infant who had the face I knew!"

* * *

I left him for a few moments to digest his tale. And then, even if I'd known about whom he'd been speaking, still I'd asked: "Who d'ye mean?"

"The Leader Of The Band," he replied, "The Dark Stranger; The Man With No Name; The Outlawed King; The Eternal Hero; Jessie James; Robin Hood; Elric Of Melnibone (I hadn't heard of him, yet!); The Buddha; The Prophet; Jesus Christ; Che Guevara; Johnny Forty Coats; Lassie; A Boy Named Sue ..."

I'd suspected all along, of course, that Herbert was behind all this, although his motives had been unclear, or, at least, beyond my comprehension. But I knew that he would have put me in this world for a purpose, and had I not been confirmed of my beliefs in the nature of, not just him, but of our mother, Mary/Maureen, too!

But what of the other world, and of Agnes? What had become of her, and it? Time there must be surely passing! But how? Could I? I asked him.

"No problem," he said, "sure isn't only right to throw the tiddlers back in!"

But first he excused himself: "Just hang on there," he said, "and I'll be right back!"

But he wasn't, or not in the way that'd I'd expected him; he'd undergone another remarkable transformation! It must have been on his way back down the stairs, that she'd caught him.

"Don't tell me," I heard her yell, "that you're off out again!" I couldn't quite catch his, whimpered, reply, but it didn't seem to please her, because she screamed:

"Always got to go somewhere, haven't you! Always got to do something, don't you! What do you do for me? What do you ever do for me?"

Again his answer, indecipherable, most have been unacceptable, because she told him then not to: "But me!" not to: "FUCKIN' BUT ME!", and brought things from bad to worse, and down along with them herself and Joseph, pounding and thumping. And unnerved me even further then, by having him re-enter the kitchen, backwards, with his hands raised to protect his skull from her hard-heeled shoe, while, with her free hand, she punched him in the stomach.

I was very embarrassed too, but didn't realise how relatively comfortable I had been, until, having left Joseph a, grovelling, pleading bundle on the floor, the white-robed spectre that was Marian, turned her attentions to me! But, sweetly, childlike even, she said: " Ooh..you are so young ... so young and innocent – aren't you boy?"

Taking it that she wasn't expecting an answer, and my frozen jaws being reluctant to let me speak, anyway, I didn't give her one. But when she said, harshly now: "Well aren't you boy?" I reckoned that a reply was in order, and, unbowing my head, I looked into her eyes and stammered: "I s-s-suppose so."

Into her eyes! Those eyes! The Green Eyes! I recognised those eyes ... Agnes eyes! Not that I'd taken an interest before in what shade they were, but I knew them; those cold, mean, bitter, angry eyes! But what were they doing in this ragged heap of a woman, who otherwise bore no resemblance?

They leered at me now, in the way that they could, and

she said: "Innocent is it boy? Don't give me your innocent! You're all the same – at any age! Sucking on our tits as soon as you're born, you should be castrated at birth, the whole lot of you!" She was starting to shout again: "Don't think I don't know what you're all like! Don't think that I don't know what you're all after! Her voice rising even higher to indicate the seriousness of the charges, it was worrying to note that the shoe rose with it. "Do you think," she threatened, "that I don't know why you're looking at me like that boy! Don't think you can fool me!" But then, as they were wont to do recently, things took a turn for the totally unexpected.

With another: "You're all the same," Marian, dropping her weapon, gripped the neck of her nightgown, and with both hands ripping it open, said: "You want these, don't you boy!"

Now Joseph's tale, initiatory as it might have been, hadn't prepared me for this, and certainly not when, without further ado, she grabbed my trembling hands, pulling me up from my seat, and placed them onto her, massively sagging, fleshy things, saying: "Go on boy, have a good feel!"

My palms, if were ever going to appreciate this kind of situation, sweaty as they were, weren't capable of it now, and they were further moistened when Marian released them, only to climb atop the shiny table, recline on her flabby elbows, tear open the rest of the gown, slide her stubby legs out either side and, indicating the hairy patch between them, said: "Well c'mon then boy, this is what you've been waiting for!"

Panicked as I was, I still had a look good enough to wonder what all the fuss was about, before Joseph's re-emergence as a physical entity saved the day.

* * *

Once again assuming more the proportions of a human-being, and less those of a discarded sack, Joseph was able to beg: "Leave him alone Marian, he's only a lad." But not with any immediate success.

"Lad, is it?" she snorted, "Don't give me lad! More like 'Jack the lad,' look at the bulge in his pants!"

There was, indeed, a lump where she spoke of, but it was, it has to be said, not due to any attractions of hers, but rather to those of my friend Jimmy, whose spare weights for his fishing rod I carried in the pockets of my shorts, in another attempt at justifying favour, I suppose. In any case, I was far to terrified to produce the swelling that she was thinking about. But then, even in the most benign of circumstances, I doubted that the sight of Marian's abandonment, stretched around the fake-fruit bowl, would have caused much of a stir down there. But, if she chose to believe differently, I certainly wasn't going to be the one to disillusion her!

In fairness to Joseph, he could but work with his assumptions, and he was making gallant efforts now to try and save me from myself. Dragging himself from the floor, he, pulling closed the window-blinds, said: "For goodness sake, will you leave it Marian! Just sit down and put some clothes on, please."

"Don't make me laugh!"she said, but it was too late; he already had: "Ha, Ha, Ha ..." she snorted. (Or, was it the familiar Agnesy version: "Ca, Ca, Ca ...?" Agnes had a problem with a problem with her palate – she'd no taste, someone had said!)

Marian laughed again, and again, until there wasn't any chance that we hadn't noticed, I presumed, before she said: "What a fraud! What a hypocrite! Do you know," she said to me, "that when I met him first all he ever wanted to do was get my clothes off. Now look at him; the free spirit, the wandering minstrel, or so he claims he could have been if it hadn't been for me, he never goes near me! But don't believe him, I never stopped him doing anything. He stayed so he could make me his private property; his wedded wife."

"That's not true," Joseph said, "anything that was done was at your behest. You're frightening the lad – that's all."

This seemed to cause Marian more mirth: "Frightening the lad? That's a good one coming from old fish features himself, going around with that stupid balaclava on your head."

"That's why he wears it," she said to me, "that, and to get up the noses of the neighbours because they objected to him playing his guitar, and revving up his stupid little motorbike at night. He walks down to the shops and all with it on, although, mostly, he uses that lousy bike."

"And do know what he calls himself? Do you know why he says that he wears that ridiculous mask? And, this is the best! Or, did he get that far? Because I'm sure he's been boring you with his silly stories too."

"He probably got it from those crappy old records that he still listens to: 'The Unknown Father,' that's what he calls himself; the unknown fuckin' father!"

"Well," she said, "I have my dreams too."

* * *

"I dream," Marian said, "of a girl, hungry and unloved, watching as a woman sits with on her knee feeding, a bastard son."

"Then of the girl again, in a room, the boy flinging her toys screaming, until the woman appears, lifts him, and stroking his head, carries him away soothing, to return to the girl scolding, slapping her, and again harder, so that she's left alone, sobbing."

"Of a schoolyard, where the likes of the boy, taunt the girl and ridicule, so that she cries the way home. To a church, where the girl with the woman stands, the boy between them, hands clasped before them, lips moving rapidly, until the boy, suddenly pale and shaking, turns and lunges through the packed bodies behind them, to where, outside, he cools his brow against the fretting stonework, and confesses to the girl, who rushed out only wishing to console him, that he, indeed, is a kinsman of Satan, a child from Hell, who has, for her, kept a place waiting."

"I dream too," said Marian, "of a comely, young maiden, lonely, waiting for a lover, only for her tower to fall to the Black Prince, who drags her screaming to his dungeon, to subject her to his most foul and excruciating of tortures. But she, courageous to the last, will not succumb to his rack and his screw, refusing to pledge herself to him and his like, but to stay always faithful to her own. And as I watch her suffer, I see that it is that girl again!"

"I dream," she says, "that she escapes and flees through the countryside, where the Black Prince now runs amok satisfying his, obscenely, depraved desires. But she, and not for revenge, but for the benefit of all her kind, swears to hunt him down and put an end to his debauched ways."

"And, so it is, that she, not due to any good fortune, but to the innate canniness of her sex, traces him to a clearing in a forest, where he and his followers gather nightly to practise their ghastly rituals and routines. But, it's as she watches on from the cover of the trees, as they, strangely attired, huddle around a campfire, mumbling their unintelligible chants, that her presence is exposed by that staunch son of Satan; that salivating supporter of the Black Prince, who, unbeknownst to her, has been shadowing her moves: The boy!"

"Pulling her into the open, they haul her, kicking and cursing, beyond the fire to a stone-made alter, where the Black Prince now stands aglow in the new light. His emissaries tethering her screaming, he slays her with his gleaming knife."

* * *

With no shimmering of lights, nor heraldic recycling, with nothing more than the raising of Joseph's eyebrows to the Heavens, I was pitched back into the other world, but, I wondered, were the scars from my capture evident? Had I been changed by my extraordinary experience? Did I appear now to be serene, calm, cool and collected, inscrutable, even? Was I a character to be reckoned with? Would people in the street mutter in respectful awe at my passing? Would dogs and smaller children follow in my train? Would the bigger ones, who didn't know who I was friendly with, stop searching me for Kate's money when I was sent to the shops, and nod reverentially instead? It seemed not! Sadly, there was even a doubt as to whether my absence had been remarked upon at all by the lads, and that time had passed with them was evidenced by three scaly friends of Joseph, glistening dead beside us. Could it really be that my disappearance had passed unnoticed?

I sought recognition from the wriggling worms, that were all that Jimmy had offered me in exchange for my, knowing, return. Skewering them more forcefully onto his hooks than was strictly necessary, it occurred to me, in the way of self-appeasement, that I could be providing fodder for the royal banquet, or, at least, for his entourage, minus Joseph; Jimmy observing that "the fuckin' fish must be havin' a fuckin' party down there Siko!"

But no, it couldn't be! Arguing a case for Mickey, as he had been, Jimmy might have been oblivious to everything else, but Roly was one of those who, no matter how distracted he might have seemed, missed nothing. I could only deduce that (In the way of these things?) I'd been sent a stand-in, although not the usual type of stuntman; but one who would sit quietly and wait, while I took all the risks! Now, as I was concerned about the hour, and hadn't yet gained the know-how to read it from the sun, was forced to refer to Roly again. He being the only one of us who you could depend on to be always wearing a watch. Which might have given him a good point, I allowed.

Unfortunately, if Jimmy had one, wherever he might have gotten it from, he couldn't have resisted for long taking the back of it, and pulling out all the fiddly bits, only to have problems getting them all back in again, or, at least, so as they'd function properly. Which leaves me an opportunity to say, that we were very different in that way: If I'd had a watch, I'd have left it alone, and not just because if it had anything to do with Kate she'd kill me for interfering with it, but because the thoughts alone of doing to mine, what Jimmy would have done to his, were enough to leave me feeling very bored. But still, that didn't save me from having to hang around with him watching Mickey do things to motorbikes other than riding them. Although, only for as long as I thought that it wasn't okay to make an excuse an go – not that I wouldn't have to be home anyway!

The worst was, when Jimmy decided to try and make himself useful, albeit in the pursuance of the most menial of tasks, and I'd be left standing there, not just fed up, but feeling totally inadequate as well, and be compelled to ask Mickey what this bit, or that bit, was for, not just to cover the fact, but to show a pretend interest as well. I always hoped that the bit I enquired of, wasn't one that should be easily recognised, by even, say, the dogs on the street, like a "carburetor," or, maybe, a "small-end bearing," and often talked about by anyone who knew anything at all about motorcycles, and that was a prerequisite to being considered cool in those days, even at my age!

I'd alway, though, add "again" when I asked, as in: "What's that bit for again, Mickey?" Just in case I was overheard, by someone other than Jimmy, and it was an obvious bit, so that it might appear that, in actual fact, I knew exactly what it was for, but it had just slipped my mind, filled as it was with thoughts bad and dangerous.

But generally, Mickey, who could get all the bits back in so as they'd function properly, would answer, if he heard me, because he mightn't, being so involved, that it was: "The overheaded-backshaft feed line for the right-sided rocker assembly," or something like that, and I'd be relieved.

Although, even when it was the carburetor he gave it to me straight, and low, so that no one else might hear.

That was the thing about Mickey; it wouldn't be: "The overheaded-backshaft feed line for the ..." with a smirking head on him, that clearly said: "Look how clever I am!" like someone of Roly's type would have done. Neither was it: "It's the carburetter, you fuckin' eejit you," again as Roly would have said. Mickey was always too busy with his own things to be bothered wondering about who was, or who wasn't, a fuckin' eejit.

He reminded me of my own brother Herbert in that way; he didn't make those kind of distinctions either. Although, in his case, it was because he realised that everyone was an eejit, really – or was it no one? Anyway, it was pointless asking him stupid questions because, knowing that you were after something more than an answer and not being able to abide that kind of dishonesty, he wouldn't reply. The only people to ask stupid questions of, I reckoned, were people who wouldn't hear them as that, being totally involved in what they were doing, like Mickey, for instance.

But Roly, on the other hand, engaged as he might be, took in everything, and tended to comment aloud on his findings too, but first he responded to my query: "It's ten minutes later than it was the last time you asked me, you stupid cunt you!" he said, "what's the problem, got to run an errand for Agnes?"

My stand-in obviously having done more than keep his own counsel, I hoped that he had told Roly to "Fuck off" too. "Fuck off Brophy, you bollocks!" I said now, and stood up as if to go, which mightn't have been very sensible, because I was left with no choice but to, when Jimmy said: " Ah sure, go ahead Siko ... you don't want to be keepin' your brother waitin'!"

So off I went, still in the dark as to the time of day. Having trudged up to the bus stop, I, after many wasted minutes, and haunted by the prospect of my still being there when the boys arrived, adopted the tactics of a heroine of one of Anna's stories; an old and very difficult one (The story, not the heroine!), who successfully attracted a procession of lifts from "kindly strangers," who took her part along her way: Sticking out my thumb, I waited, impatiently, for someone kindly to come my way.

* * *

The kindly people must have all stayed home that day, leastways the ones with the cars, or so I was believing when enough of them had passed me by, that I, having lost faith in both human nature and the country's public transport system, deserted my post, and, with my thumb still waving, began, what I feared, would be the long march home. But it was my concerns about the future that caused me to fail to see the beast of the past looming, large, behind me!

Slipping, slowing, beyond me, it halted darkly snarling, daring me to venture over and peer into it's murky entrails. But boldly hasten across I did, and, more so, climbed into the body of the beast, to be restrained by an unseen force as, with a roar, it bounded forwards. Warmly, drowsily, in it's clutches I sat, speechlessly, enjoying the ride, until from beside me, the beast-master, the driver of the Jaguar, demanded: "What brought you this way, son?" Not wishing to converse, but recognising it as the price to be paid by the successful hitch-hiker I, stifling a yawn, answered: "Fishin'! At the lakes down there!" Chancing a look at him as I pointed, I couldn't, through the haze of his cigarette smoke, be certain of anything but the large moustache that should have left the rest of his face unremarkable even on a clear day; a cousin of the type that languished around the bars and bookies' shops on a Saturday afternoon; a brother to the ones worn by the guys in the films, who were never up to any good!

But catching my glance with a sinister laugh, he said: "You'd want to be careful son, there's some strange people about in these parts."

* * *

For my obligatory, "Is that right?" I was rewarded with a: "When I was a young fella', although older than you are now, meself and a few mates went campin' down this way. A few miles back there," he said, aiming the cigarette over his shoulder.

"We hadn't got a proper tent that first night", he said "but we were going to get one the next day, there was always enough gobshites around who went off and left theirs standin', we'd only a bit of canvass that we stuck up with a few branches."

"It pissed rain that night, and I think that we must have camped in a river-bed, because we were drowned out of it. So we upped and found ourselves a hay-barn. We dug in, and I have to say it was fuckin' great! Warm and dry it was, and I was havin' a grand ol' kip for meself. But I was disturbed by one of the lads, Anto, callin' 'Ronnie! Ronnie! Are ye awake? Can ye hear it?'"

"Now I couldn't hear anything other than his blatherin', and really pissed off I was with him for waking me up, so I told him to shut up and go back to fuckin' sleep, or I'd break every bone in his body. But I couldn't go back to sleep, and as I lay there pickin' bits of hay from me ears, and up me nostrils and out of me jockey's, I heard it."

"As well as being wet that night it was also wild, and every now and again the wind would gust and I could pick it up. And it got clearer, especially after I'd given Anto a good toe up the back to stop his snorin'. Music! But not the diddli-idle stuff that the culchies only listen to."

"So, I told Anto to stop his moanin', and to come with me and we'd check it out. We didn't bother letting the others know because they were buried deep and, anyway, even if we could find them, we mightn't be able to wake the stupid cunts; I'll say this much for Anto, apart from me, he was the only one of us who could handle his gargle."

"But it was pitch black, and we'd only the music to guide us, but it was so weird that we thought it must be worth following; we reckoned there'd have to be some mad party, or even an orgy, at the source of it! The ground was swampy, twice I went out on my back, and so did Anto – I brought him with me – so that by the time we saw the lights, we were really manky."

"They were comin' from this cottagy place that you'll always come across in the arsehole of nowhere, but they were blazin' and the music was blarin', so Anto wanted to go right up and bang on the door. But, I wasn't on for it: the state of us! I didn't want some crazy farmer chasin' me back across the fields with his shotgun. So, instead, we snuck up to one of the windows and had a peek in. But I says to Anto: 'Some fuckin party! Some fuckin' orgy you've brought me to!' Because there in this room, sittin' on a bed, was a bloke; well we thought it was a bloke, we couldn't see that much of him because there were curtains on the window, even if they weren't closed properly. But if it was a woman, from what I could see, she looked to have a pair of size twelve feet, and a fine pair of balls on her. And you know what was beside him?"

I wasn't quick enough to hazard a guess.

"A record player," Ronnie said, "a fuckin' record-player!"

" 'Fuck this for a game of cowboys,' I says to Anto, 'some fuckin' orgy – a bloke on his todd with a record player!' "

"But," Ronnie said, "we'd gone to a lot of trouble to get there, so we were going to have a suss over the rest of the place before we left. At the next window Anto, runt that he was, just made for stickin' his nose into other people's business, looks in first, and says: 'Jaysus Ronnie, have a gander at this, will ye!' But the little wanker wouldn't get out of me way, so I had to give him a smack on the head and a boot in the arse, before I could get in and have a good geek in the window. I could see why he didn't want to move! There's a mot in there with not a dicky on her, and she's not on her own either; beneath her, on the bed, there's this baldy oul fella', and she's bouncin' off him as if there's no tomorrow, tits and hair flyin everywhere."

"But Anto's up off the ground, and he starts sniggerin' in me ear, and she must have heard him, because she stops humpin' the oul fucker and stares right over at the window to where we were. Now we could have legged it, well Anto might have done, but she must have been wide to that, because she signs us to wait. And we did. So would anyone, if they'd have seen her!"

* * *

"We waited outside," Ronnie said, "while she went around to open the door for us. Bollock naked she still was too! I could have got up on her there and then, but she leads us into a room where there's a table covered with sandwiches and cakes and biscuits and stuff, and tells us that she has to go somewhere, but to help ourselves and that she'll be back soon."

"We got stuck into the grub: we were starvin'; we hadn't eaten that day, only drank! The music had stopped, and we'd heard an engine starting, and it was quiet then, so we reckoned that yer man and the baldy oul fella must have gone too. But we weren't in the mood for touchin' anything other than herself, so we stayed where we were, until, sure enough, we heard a motor pulling in, and our door swings open and she's standin' there, in just a pair of black knickers and a pair of high-heels now, playin' with her tits, and askin': 'Who's first? Or would you prefer to come together?'

"Now," he said, "I had a horn on me that would pull an elephant out of a swamp, but while I'm chokin' on me jammy doughnut, Anto slips in with a 'ME!' and makes a dive for her."

"So she takes him by the hand, smiles back, and says she'll see me later. I couldn't believe her!" he said, "I couldn't see her being that long: Anto was such an ugly little bastard that he'd be lucky to get his hole in a brothel. He'd be so excited that he'd probably come in his trousers. But I was wrong, they were ages."

"I was really fed up, especially when that horrible music started again. I felt like goin' in and jumpin' all over yer man and his record-player, but I didn't, and only because she mightn't have liked it. I couldn't imagine what they'd be doin' that was keepin' them so long: Anto wouldn't have a clue what to do, and if she tried anything weird, that's if he knew the difference, he'd run screaming. But, when he did come running, it wasn't for any reason that I'd expected."

"It had occurred to me that the bastards had fallen asleep and forgotten all about me and, furious, I'd just gotten off my chair to go in to them, when Anto appeared in front of me with his shirt and his trousers half on him, hoppin' up and down, and shoutin', 'Let's get the fuck outa here! Let's go!' So I gave him a slap across the mouth, and said: 'Where's the fire? What's the fuckin' story ... Rory?"

"But he's roaring: 'She's a fuckin' spacer! ... a fuckin' nut! She wants us to bring us up a fuckin' mountain and leave us with a load of other nuts. She wants to save us!'"

"Now," Ronnie said, "if there's one kind of nut I never could stand, it's a religious nut – actin' as if they're so much better than everyone else."

"When we were kids," he explained, "there was an empty old house where we used to play, until a gang of them came along and took it over. Every night they'd be in there, readin' their bibles and singin' and playin' their guitars. We'd slag them off when they were coming and going, and throw bricks at their windows, when they were inside, but they wouldn't react, they were useless; they wouldn't chase us or anything, just kept fixin' the fuckin' windows as if we didn't matter, as if we didn't mean a fuckin' thing to them, at all."

"But they got their comeuppance," he said, " they were seen talking to some of the younger kids, and word got around that the religion thing was all bollocks; that really they were drug dealers and child molesters, they were finished then! The kids fathers got together and went up one night, dragged them all outside and beat the livin' shit out of them, and warned them that if they ever saw them around again they'd be crucified. There was no room for perverts in our neighbourhood!"

"So, of course," he said, "when I heard that she wanted to 'Save' us, something clicked in me head. She came up behind Anto and put her hand on his shoulder, and I completely freaked. I pushed him out of the way and kicked her between the legs. She screamed, and so she should have done, I was wearin' me new 'George Webbs,' covered in fuckin' muck they were now as well, and fell to the floor. But the music kept playin', so I reckoned that yer man next door hadn't heard, so I kicked her again, but this time in the stomach, and she wails so loud then that the music does stop."

"Anto grabs the table and tips it over, plates and everything smashing over her, and we turn to leg it."

"But yer man, the music man, big fucker that he is, is there blockin' our way. With a black balaclava on him only showin' his mouth and eyes, like he's a fuckin' terrorist or something! He tries to get a grip of me, but, luckily, me being a skin back then, his hand slips off me head. Now I wasn't goin' to take him on, not with just a short-arsed fucker like Anto with me, so when he comes at me again, I makes a dive for the floor, but yer woman, still down there, beside me, screams: 'Let them go! Let them go! Vengeance shall be his!' "So he steps aside, and off we go."

"We ran and we ran, and we fell and we ran, and we didn't know where the fuck we were runnin' to, and every now and again, on the wind, we could still here her screamin': 'Vengeance shall be his,' and by the time we found the barn, it was mornin'."

"Now, of course, we told the rest of them about what had happened, and even though they wouldn't believe us, they still wanted to go and burn the place down anyway; they were very loyal like that!"

"But, to be honest with you, I never wanted to see that house again. And Anto must have been the same, because we shut up about it, and the other lads still would have thought that we'd been spoofing, so they didn't mention it either. But that wasn't the end of it." he said.

"No?"I said.

"No," he answered, "one day, back in Dublin, meself and Anto were crossing a road, and it was quiet, there was fuck all traffic, when from nowhere, and I mean nowhere, this jeep thing suddenly appears, and it's bearin' right down on us. I made a jump for it and just about got clear, I think there was paint from the jeep on the heels of me docs, but poor Anto wasn't quick enough, not this time, and I could hear him screamin' as it rolled over him."

"When I looked around he was lyin' on the road, his face all messy with blood, and his body twitching. The jeep did stop then, but only for long enough for the driver to turn and smile back at us. And d'ye know who it was?"

Like poor Anto, I wasn't quick enough!

"It was yer woman," he said, "the mad bitch from the cottage! Then she fucked off again."

"And Anto?" I asked. "Did he die?"

"Not straightaway," Ronnie said, "but he was brain-damaged,

which a lot of people thought was very funny, because they said that he'd never had one anyway. But he'd become a total moron now, couldn't speak properly or anything, we used to give him an awful slaggin', until he fell under a bus and put an end to it all."

"Did you ever find her?" I asked.

"No," he said, "we found the house but it was deserted, and the people around said that, as far as they knew, it had been for years. They hadn't known anything about her, or her boyfriend. But I'm still lookin'," he said, "I'm still lookin' for her and hers. And there's strange people about in these parts."

* * *

Still, I managed to fall asleep in Ronnie's car – I must have done, because he was waking me up when we got to the park.

"Well here ye are son," he was saying, "off you go now and I'll be seein' ye around," as I gratefully took my leave.

It was quieter in the park than it might have been, and I wasn't aware of any kids by whom I'd be recognised, so I did a circuit of the football pitches and the tennis courts, before heading for the playground. Checking out the swings and the roundabouts, I even had a go on the slides, in an attempt, I told myself, to heighten my profile. I slid on my backside, and then on my belly which, as it transpired, took a turn for the painful: I having neglected to remove Jimmy's spare weights from my pockets. Uttering curses fouler than my usual; it must have been from hanging around with Ronnie, I pulled them out, Kate's old watch fell to the ground.

Kate's old watch fell to the ground! What was I doing with Kate's old watch? Or, as I put it at the time: "What the fuck is Kate's old fuckin' watch doin' in my fuckin' pocket?" Hadn't

Anna said that Agnes had taken it with her the night before! I sat down to try and figure it out, but only for as long it took two dangerous looking eight year olds to warn me of the dire consequences of not shifting rapidly from their slide. So, capable of it still, and with no need yet for an anal toothbrush, I wandered into the forest and re-parked myself, relatively comfortably, on a bumpy patch of ground.

Seemingly, the short walk had cleared my head, for it was obvious to me now: Ronnie had planted it on me! Ronnie had pushed the watch into my pocket while I'd been sleeping! But what had he done with Agnes, and why? Surely she was one of "theirs!" and not of "hers!" A professed enemy of Herbert's and of mine, and so, in consequence, of our mother Mary/Maureen, or Jezebel, or any other names by which she'd been known; Agnes was on the bad side!

Stumbling over this paradox, my mind switched off and went to sleep again, to awake only after nightfall, the blackness pure; undiluted by any moon or star-shine.

"Fuck this for a game of soldiers," I said, removing my back from a tree trunk. But, I wasn't too concerned, not really, other than about what Kate would do to me when I got home. Like anyone else who scrambled their way along at night behind enemy lines, my eyes would soon adjust to the darkness. But it didn't happen for me as quickly as I'd expected.

Smacking my head against a low bough, I tripped over the rooty bits, my clothes caught on some scraggly ends and my foot fell into a rabbit hole? I slid down a hillside and landed in some dogshite? I should have asked Jimmy for a few of his matches before I left him! I should have eaten my carrots when I was told to!

I should have had a torch strapped around my "middle" with a pen-knife and a compass attached, same as other young adventurers would have had. I should have had a ball of twine and a comb for my hair. I should have had some sticking plaster and a tin of sardines. I should have had my lucky rabbit's foot and a picture of the Pope. I should have had a ham sandwich and a waterproof "mac".

I should have had respect for my elders and an aptitude for games. I should have been stronger, brighter and better-looking, and be a credit to the people who reared me. I should have known what I wanted to be when I grew up. I should have wanted to grow up!

I should have felt like a commando now, and not like a character who's lost in a maze: I could picture him; skipping in, smiling, as if he hadn't got a "care in the world," strolling about, with his hands in his pockets, like he has it all sussed. Until, in time, the smile wears thin and he becomes panicky; his eyes are darting about in his head now and his hands are out of his pockets, he's running around shouting for help, but no one hears him, and he collapses in a corner: a broken old man. That film always bothered me. Or was it a dream?

But I wouldn't panic, not now! If I couldn't find my way out soon, I'd be bound to find a soft spot where I could hole up for the night – Kate could only kill me once! I wasn't going to start crying out; I had to live with myself! And, more to the point, I might have to live near to whoever it was who'd come to rescue me, and credibility was hard enough to come by in those days. Anyway, the dark held no great fears for me. And, so it was, that it was the coming of the light that terrified me.

* * *

It was a white light, the kind that Jimmy's brother Mickey used when he was working on his motorbike. It dazzled me, and made the trees indoors as it channelled a passageway between them. I took my hands from my eyes and followed the route that it was charting, feeling a bit like I did went to the pictures on a Saturday morning with Jimmy and Roly, except, here, I couldn't spot the usher, and when I did find my seat, I was alone apart from the remaining light.

An invisible voice ordering me to "Sit!" I did, but only after examining the chair for stains beforehand, because it was the schoolroom type, and we shared ours with a lad with acute kidney problems, so if anyone had been cruel enough to shift the "O'Brien" seat, woe betide he who landed upon it; the slagging could be awful! It had become as much of a habit for me to check a seat before I sat on it, as it was to look under a bed before I got into it, and I reckoned that I might be doing that for the rest of my life, if I lived that long!

But it wasn't the only thing from the classroom: There before me was a screen, suspended from the sky, it seemed to be, identical to the one that they used to show us anti-smoking and whatever-else-was-fun films, or, to educate us on, maybe, 'The Workings of the Canadian Grain Industry,' or, 'The Benefits of Proper Dental Care'. Sometimes it showed a western, or even a war film, but only outside school hours, and we were supposed to pay in.

But now, I couldn't help feeling as excited as I always did when the light faded, the film rolled, and the screen hissed and splattered into life, with it's splodges and it's disjointed countdown. Even when it was only, 'The Workings of the Canadian Grain Industry,' or, 'The Benefits of Proper Dental Care,' we'd often clap and cheer. So, I was told to: "Stop fidgeting, fold my arms and pay attention," before the man with no shirt roared (The man with no shirt roared?), and 'HELION PRODUCTIONS' brought us: 'The Girl with no

Hands,' or was it ... 'The Girl with no Palms'? 'The Girl with no Qualms'... that must have been it! I didn't quite catch the opening title as I was busy picking my nose, or, more critically, disposing of it's contents.

We began: "Dum, Dum, De, Dum, Dum, Dum," I'd never be able to hear that type of music without it reminding me of old films, and we're in a forest.

"Dum, Dum, Dum," there's a girl hiding behind a tree. It's Agnes! It's not... it's Marian! No, it's definitely Agnes; it was just my imagination!

She's made visible to us by the light of a camp-fire, where around stand a group of masked men.

"Dum, Dum, Dum," she creeps nearer, "Dum, Dum, De, Dum, Dum," and leans forward, "Dum, Dum, Dum, Dum," in an attempt, it seems, to catch the words that are spilling from their lips.

"FHOOTTT," she farts. "Dum, Dum, Dum, De, Dum, Dum, Dum, Dum, Dum, Dum, De, Dum, Dum, Dum," they chase her back into the forest, and catch her, "Dum. Dum, Dum," dragging her screaming, "Dum, Dum, Dum, Dum," to the alter that has just appeared in the scene.

Behind the alter stands a cowboy-hatted figure, very loud "Dums," with clashes: "Tssssa, Tsssa," who as they hold her down, pronounces: "For what you have said! For what you have done! For what you have not failed to do!" And nods to a knife-wielding accomplice who, "Dum, Dum, Dum, Screech, Screech, Dum, Dum, Screech," slays her with his eyes agleam. The screen blanked. The audience applauded.

PART TWO

1977

Herbert disappeared for a while after that, but of his own free will, and not because of Ronnie's dastardly plot to implicate him in the killing of Agnes. Strangely, they said they hadn't been able to come across her dead or alive, and so couldn't blame him for either. For my own part, I refused to tell of what I had seen, realising that to do so would be to fall into Ronnie's trap and, because of his cunning impersonation, bear witness against Herbert, and not him. I didn't as much as mention it to Jimmy! Still, it was a good effort by the Black Prince, and he'd be bound to try again, and as it was said that he could take on many guises, and surely wouldn't announce what they were, we would have to be on our guard. But, I could only be thankful to him for choosing Agnes as his sacrifice, although, I'll have to admit, the house was very quiet without her.

Anna would hardly speak to me at all. She went out a lot, and when she was in, and she wasn't busy with anything else, she read even more, or, stared at the walls again. In retaliation?

I read more myself, having happened upon some books about German soldiers in the Second World War who spent most of their time on the Eastern Front, and so familiarised me enough with hardship and deprivation, that I could stand at the bus-stop, in the worst of winter, without a coat on.

Disappointingly though, I'd found them in a second-hand bookshop and not along with the music that Herbert had left me, when he'd vacated my room. He didn't appear to have read any books, but that was because, I believed, no one had written one good enough for him, or, he'd read everything worth reading, before he was aged about ten.

Kate went to seed (whatever that means?). She left her job and took to lying on the couch all day, drinking and taking valium. I'd taken to drinking, and sometimes taking valium with it too, but rarely at home. Bitch and all that Agnes had been, Kate was still very upset by her going. Fortunately Anna, as well as doing practically all of the housework, got a part-time job, and then, when she upped and left school, a full-time one. I think that's how we survived!

And her job must have paid very well because, having acquired a boyfriend, she was able to get a telephone in, so that they, she having so much to do, could still talk when they couldn't see each other, or, so that he, could leave messages, when she wasn't there, but then, only if I was, because Kate would never answer it. It was absolutely no advantage to me, not knowing anyone else that had a telephone, apart from Roly Brophy, that is, and I wasn't going to ring him!

The trouble with this arrangement was that her boyfriend wasn't the only one who'd ring. Someone else would too. Someone who I really didn't like the sound of, who wouldn't give his name, so that I'd have to tell him to "Fuck off!" and then, when he'd ring back, pretending to be someone different, I'd do the same again. But it got to the stage where I had to tell almost everyone who rang for Anna to "Fuck off!" – even the girls, just in case he'd put them up to it!

It led, of course, to me being threatened once or twice, but then I'd tell of who I knew, even feeling justified in mentioning "The Gibneys," who were market leaders in intimidation back then: some of Mickey's friends, who were really rough, often spoke of them. I told Charlie, Anna's boyfriend, to "Fuck Off!" a couple of times too, but I think he understood. Anna stayed at home more often.

Charlie would often call to the house. He was okay really; he looked very scholarly with his big spots and glasses, but he didn't bore you with it. He was quiet, or, at least, he realised that we wouldn't have a lot in common. If we were waiting together for Anna, he'd pick up a newspaper and act as if he was reading it; it could be Kate's tabloid, surely of no interest to him, while I'd make a show of watching TV. Kate, herself, would usually be too far gone from us, even in the earlier parts of the day, to interfere.

Sometimes, maybe to make him feel more comfortable, or, to remind him that I didn't dislike him, I'd offer him a cigarette, as if I'd forgotten that he'd told me that he didn't smoke or drink, or give the impression that he got into fights either, but he'd always tell me again, as if it was the first time that it had happened. Our only mistake was when I tried him on football, and he pretended to be interested, so that, if he came in now while I was watching a match, he'd feel obliged to make annoying remarks about "magnificent stadiums" and "wonderful goals," but otherwise we got on.

Anyway, if she was there, he'd usually be up with Anna in her bedroom, she having it all to herself now that Agnes had gone, discussing difficult books or playing chess: I couldn't imagine what else they'd be doing; Anna wouldn't have been interested in him in that way! But, even if they were doing anything else – which they definitely weren't! – Kate wouldn't have complained, being the way that she was now, and that's how I got out so much myself.

Usually, I'd be down with Jimmy, and with Mickey and his friends, and he had some even tougher- looking new ones; it seemed that all of them had been in prison, if only the junior versions, and they talked about "strokin' " all the time. But they never did more with us other than drink and play cards, and Jimmy's father would join in too. Patrick wouldn't, of course, especially now that he was going to become a priest, but he rarely complained, and it was fun, for the most part, until Mickey was killed.

* * *

I was first to him: On my way from Kate's house to theirs, he appeared "pulling wheelies" in front of me. I marveled at his control when, on lifting his front wheel from the road, he took a hand of the bars and waved it clear beside him, especially now that he was on a six-fifty, and not one of the lesser things that he'd had beforehand. But then, when again at the peak of his balancing act, I heard a screech, and from behind me a car came tearing, and ploughed through both man and machine.

I rushed over to the wreckage, and distinguishing Mickey's features from amongst it, knelt to catch his dying words. He kissed me (?), and said: "I'm hit! I'm hit! They got me kid! The bastards have got me!"

I'd little memory of the car, but still had recognised it as a small Fiat, and not the great Jaguar of the Prince. But someone, somewhere, had noted part of the registration; stolen. It had read: "Something, Something, Something, URI." "Something, Something, Something, You Or I!" The Black Prince had thrown down the gauntlet.

* * *

But how apt for him to seek his revenge thus. What divine symmetry (somewhere in Herbert's records, I think?). Hadn't his sidekick, Anto, been despatched in a similar way! What better now than to strike back at the brother of the friend of Mary's other son! The Black Prince was on the warpath and, in Herbert's absence, it was for me to stand alone. But how could I contend with his powers? How could I gauge where and when he would next attack? If only I could take the fight to him! But, how? Surely, it was impossible! But then there was an occurrence that gave me hope.

Anna came home unusually quiet. Unusually, because not possessing, and choosing not to possess, Agne's capacity for destroying a comfortable atmosphere, she was still too much of a female to completely conceal her mood. I asked her what was wrong, and was she sure, but she refused to say, and retired to her room. I just assumed that she'd had a row with Charlie, maybe even finally broken up, especially when he didn't appear the next day, and it was so unlike him to miss a Sunday. Strangely, it wasn't until I went into school again that I learnt the real story.

Anna and Charlie, who both attended ours, were active members of the local amateur dramatic group. This could mean meeting three or more times weekly, to familiarise themselves with roles that they'd perform but once or twice yearly, in the local community hall. But, even though there would be few outside their immediate families (include me out!), and a usual assortment of captive pensioners who went to see them, they might still be invited "down the country" in the summertime, to play to like-minded groups, acting as if they appreciated them.

Now, apart from Charlie, there were others from our school who were involved. Although, mostly in the senior years, there were some, like one in our class, who wasn't an actor, but whose brother was, who helped with the props when he was needed, especially when they were out of town. Matthew was his name, and this is, more or less, what he told me.

On the day in question, the group had put on a matinee show for their rural hosts and so were free to travel back early enough, they being a theatre group, to organise flasks and goodies for a picnic along the way. Selecting what they considered to be a suitable spot: short green grass and no threatening scenery, they settled themselves down, joyfully, to feast on their cucumber sandwiches cut sideways, and discuss the least controversial works of Shakespeare. But then Charlie, probably having done the dog on the Miwadi, urgently felt the need to have a piss, or, in their speak: "to use the loo," and was forced to dislodge himself from the jollities, and set off to find it.

As they'd situated themselves about the centre of a large field he, being the modest chap that he certainly was, made for the cover of some trees over at the furthest end of it to do his business, so it was no surprise to anyone when he wasn't back in a hurry. In truth, it's doubtful that it was even noticed that he was gone at all, except maybe by Anna, and so it was, that it was she who raised the alarm, but only after they'd re-jarred their pickles and folded up their napkins, and he still hadn't returned.

Showing the tenacity of their amateurly dramatic allegiance, and not because they'd miss his gutteral tones for "Yis are all very quiet up the front," on the bus on the way home, these conscientious, mostly young folk, promptly organised and made to find him. And did they!

Charlie, not being one for the limelight, had never, in their performances to date, shown any ambition to play but the minutest of roles, considering his interests as being more in the directorial sphere. But now, completely unexpectedly, he'd found himself promoted "in the field," the leading man he'd become, a creature of nightmares!

Bound and gagged, and stripped naked from the waist down, arms and legs splayed wide, he was lashed to a tree in the severest of fashions. But that wasn't the worst of it for him, the tragedy was, that it didn't seem to bother him at all; for when the shocked crowd gathered around to observe him, it couldn't but be noticed, that his little thing stood up and stared right back at them. No amateur show; surely another production from Hell!

Not far away, on a fence sat sniggering, was a bunch of doc-martined and denim uniformed skinheads, indistinguishable from each other to the naked eye, except to our narrator Matthew, who recognised one of them as being an ex-neighbour and schoolmate of his and mine: my old foe Roly Brophy!

* * *

Okay, I'll admit it was along shot, but I'd nothing else to go on, and, anyway, the more I thought about it, the more convinced I became: Hadn't Ronnie said that he'd been a skinhead too, and didn't the Charlie incident, according to Matthew, occur within only a stone's throw – if not by someone like myself – of our fishing spot, which was itself, and I had Ronnie's word for this, in close proximity to the Mary house. Wasn't it quite conceivable that Roly, having become a whimpering lacky of the Black Prince, was now abetting him in his quest for retaliation on "her and hers," hence the attack on poor Charlie, who, unwittingly, had gotten himself loosely connected. Well it was believable to me, and there was no one else who I had to convert!

Which led me to further thinking on the subject, and the realisation that Roly was one of those in the forest the night Agnes was slain, possibly even the wielder of the knife himself: They never got on; they called each other "fat" things. There really was no love lost between them, which was all that I'd had in common with both.

And Roly had gone to Hell, everyone said so! They said they didn't know what had come over him, but it was looking likely that he'd disappoint his mother, and not even follow in his father's engineering footsteps, if, personally, I'd always seen him as becoming something much more exciting, like a school inspector or a rent man. But, the way he was behaving now, they: Aunt Bridgit and a few other voices, said that he was going to find himself in a lot of trouble when he stopped being a skinhead.

His family had left us to move to a 'better' area, mostly to get him away from the Conroys, I would have assumed, but the stories kept coming back. The gist of them was his ongoing refusal to take to his new environment and his relationship with a neighbouring one, notable for it's production of skinheads, like the one that he himself had become, famed for their ten-strong attacks on singletons, and the stealing of blind ladies old handbags. I knew; I'd had trouble with them myself! Not with Roly's band, or "Rolo," as they apparently called him now, but with another crew, whose own notoriety was due in no small part to the fearless beating-up and strangling of stray cats, and the kicking of people in the head and the taking then of their "Wrangler" jackets, which was exactly what had happened to me!

It was true that Jimmy and myself dressed in the same way as they did: Wrangler jackets, Wrangler "wides" and Doc Martin boots, but, otherwise, we'd retained our individuality. For instance: I had longish dark hair, whereas Jimmy had shortish fair hair, and sometimes a new friend of Jimmy's, called Rayo, would be with us, and he had a bright red head. It was said that Rayo had strangled cats too, but then he had been very disturbed.

And Jimmy's doc's were two-toned! He'd left them ox-blood on the sides and dyed them black down the middle. I'd tried to do the same with mine, but had made a mess of it, and then wore them out in the rain before they'd dried, so that now they were a kind of smudgy purple. I really should have left them to Jimmy, who'd gotten to be especially good at stuff like that, now that Mickey had been killed. I wasn't sure about Patrick, because he'd never had any bikes or Doc Martins.

I wasn't one of those people then, who were wearing safety pins through their noses. That was only for the "Poshies" who we chased through town in the summertime, and the kind of absolute lunatic that no one would dare say a word to, anyway! But I did like the music. Herbert had been gone so long that, as well as listening to his, I'd gone and brought in some of my own. Although, I was sure that he would have approved, especially of the Sex Pistols album. I'd had that before they even covered up "The Bollocks." Anna liked it too, and arrived home with the loan of the Stranglers one (I don't know who else she knew?): "Do, Do, Do, - De, Do, De, Do, Do," I could have listened to it all day! But then Anna always had good taste in music, unlike Agnes who'd, of course, been into The Osmonds before she'd disappeared.

Which has brought me away from the skinheads, and the night that they kicked me in the head. I went straight to Conroys afterwards, but only Jimmy's father was with him, and although he wanted to come with us, we'd insisted that he stayed. But, thankfully, we weren't able to find any, and, on the way home, Jimmy said that we'd just have to "let the hare sit." I agreed, and then asked him what he'd meant the next day. He told me that he didn't really know, but was sure that he'd meant the type that people shot in the countryside, and not the ones on your head. I'd laughed, and added that that was certainly the case now, as it was a bunch of skinheads that we were dealing with.

But the hare stood up and scratched himself!

* * *

Ronnie wasn't the only Prince who was around then, if only according to the man who'd appeared to be the other one's father. They were into Elvis down in Conroy's, well some of them were anyway, and they played him all the time, which was all very well, except for their singing along.

Jimmy's father would stand up with a beer bottle, preferably an empty one so that he couldn't spill any, push his bit of hair back, made easier by the amount of grease he still tried to wear in it, and then, after peering deep into the bottle, place his hand at the back of his neck, jiggle his lips and shout hoarsely in Scottish (Any resemblances to Elvis were surely imperceptible!): "Since ma baby left ..." or, "It's a one for the money, it's a two for the show ..." and Jimmy, sitting beside me, would bang his heels on the floorboards, put his hands flat on his knees, wave them in and out and join in the chorus, cleverly switching Elvis's (Or did he borrow it from someone else?) footwear for his own, as in: "Oh Siko don't you step on my two-tone docs ..." which was very awkward, unless I was "locked out of my head," as well.

Jimmy's father called Patrick "The Prince" because he thought that he was the image of Elvis, but it was only after Elvis died that he told us that Patrick actually was his son. There was little doubt about it, he said. He'd checked through Elvis's known itinerary and discovered that he had been vacationing at a secret destination around the time of Patrick's conception, and as Patrick's mother had been leaving home most evenings then, to, supposedly, tend to her own sick one, as he put it himself: "Ye wudnae ha' to be friggin' Ian Stein to work da un ooot!"

Supporting his conviction, was his memory of the lady as another Elvis fan, they had had there good times together, he'd often concede, and as a whore, coupling together, making him, for her, an irresistible target. That's why he didn't blame Elvis; hadn't he been caught the same way himself! Only Elvis hadn't been fool enough to hang around and jeopardise, nay sacrifice, his career, as he had done with Glasgow Celtic and Scotland.

But, at the end of the day, not even Elvis could escape the clutches of women, and so it was that they had brought him to his grave. You could tell that, Jimmy's father said, from listening to his songs; you never heard him singing about drugs. And let not anyone say different in his "hoos"!

Patrick was going to become a priest, he said, for that very same reason. Even if he wasn't aware of it himself, his prime motivation was the avoidance of women, in deference to the fates of his fathers. He displayed the signs of making a very modest priest too, because, when Jimmy's father broke the news to him, he seemed completely calm and unmoved, and showed no interest in claiming his inheritance, that is, if bastards had any rights in Elvis's part of the world?

But, although he was another man's child, Jimmy's father had never held it against him. It was, he said, such a privilege for him to live under the same roof as the son of "The King" - that's why he called Patrick "The Prince", he explained to us then - it was just a pity that his mother hadn't confessed, and early enough for him to have christened him "Elvis Junior," and Presley was, indeed, a good Scottish name. He'd only discovered the truth after she'd left him, but it had helped him through the ensuing years.

I'd never let on, but I couldn't see the resemblance. Patrick had black hair and a harelip (Or, was that just due to recent conversations with Jimmy?), but after that....? The truth was, I didn't take much notice of Patrick, not even when he picked things up, or dusted, around me. Agnes always said that Patrick was queer, even before I knew what that meant, but still, I didn't ask Jimmy! But, all in all, Patrick didn't bother me, not even for going to be a priest. I couldn't imagine him as the usual type; telling you what you could and couldn't do, and insisting on being called "Father" – no-one could seriously call Patrick that! And, anyway, I'd thought about it, and decided that in my fight against the other prince, it might be no harm to have a priest in my corner. It was after Mickey was killed that I got the opportunity to talk to him about it.

* * *

I didn't make much use of it though! It was as if most of the neighbours came back to Conroy's house after Mickey was killed, pretending to be upset, but really delighted to be rid of him and his friends and motorbikes. I was convinced that they actually only came for the free food and drink, but I got there first: I'd felt very unwell during the mass again, so I ran out early, and had already taken up position in the kitchen when Patrick came out for the tea and sandwiches.

Catching him at the sink, I broached my subject: "Do you think he's in Hell?"

He swung around and said: "Oh, hello Billy,"(he refused to call me Siko!) "what was that you asked me?"

"Mickey," I said, "I mean, I know that he was a sound bloke and all, you couldn't get better! But he smoked and drank, and rode loads of women; do you not think he'd be gone to Hell now?"

Patrick would surely make it as a priest, because he stood there the way that they could; as if contemplating matters too spiritual for the layman. In fact, he was so good at it that I was thinking that I'd have to ask him again, when he unclasped his hands, straightened his neck and said:

"What is Hell, Billy?"

Now I was quiet for a bit myself after that, but I imagined that I wouldn't have appeared to be very spiritually contemplative: I was seriously irritated! I hated when they played those kind of games, and only for who Patrick was who he was, I might have told him so. If he, who was about to become a priest, couldn't say what Hell was, then what chance for the rest of us? But maybe he'd given me the opening I'd been looking for.

"Hell," I said, "with the Devil, or whatever you call him: Satan; Beelzebub; Lucifer; The Bringer of Light; The Prince of Darkness; The Corrupter of the Flesh; The Enemy of God and of his Son; The Enemy of his Son's Brother; The Enemy of his Son's Brother's Friends; The Enemy of his Son's Brothers Friends Brothers; The Stealer of Cars; The Player of Cards ..."

"Well," said Patrick, "If that's where he is, maybe he's in the proper company at last," and swung away again."

It was such a strong ending for the scene, that I couldn't but leave it at that. But still, I hadn't minded being in the kitchen alone with Patrick. I didn't even keep my back against the wall, the way everyone would have said that I should: Patrick wasn't queer, indeed, he was another one who was chasing Anna, even if she wasn't into Elvis.

He called regularly to see Kate after Agnes went. Of course, he'd ask for Kate and claim that he was around to offer his support, or condolences. But Anna was the real purpose of his visits; I could tell by the way he looked at her. Although, not in her room, she wouldn't allow him that!

Not that I would have minded him being with Anna, he being a Conroy, and this before Charlie was around, she could have done a lot worse! She could have been with someone like Roly Brophy, whom she insisted on saying hello to, and smiling back at, no matter what I said! And even when she found out for herself: that "Poor Charlie" episode, the sickeningly familiar voice still came on the phone. But it was only after they got Patrick too, and Herbert came back, that we set out to get him.

* * *

Patrick was on his way home, from late-night shopping, I supposed, when he was set upon by the same bunch of skinheads that had caught me. They'd known who he was too; there was no doubt that it wasn't premeditated, because once when, from behind a high wall, Jimmy and myself had thrown bottles at them, climbing it, they'd shouted after us: "We'll get you Conroy! You and your arse-bandit of a brother!" And Patrick had had no Wrangler jacket!

He came out worse than I did; I'd been cute enough to roll myself into a ball, put my hands over my head and then run at the earliest opportunity. But he was, of course, too naive for that, having never hung around. They broke his nose, rattled his teeth and caused him to be housebound for days, leaving Jimmy stuck with the messages.

Saturday evening, about a week later, having first shared a few of her vodkas, without Kate, I went down to Conroy's to meet up with the rest of them. It being customary now for us to drink on at least two weekend nights, and on a Wednesday too, if we could afford it, just to break up the week. I wasn't working like Jimmy, but it was rarely I'd hadn't got a line going in the likes of grass-cutting or charity-box collecting. Mickey's old Honda 50, Jimmy had, indeed, inherited it, was very familiar with our jaunts to and from the off-licence.

I'd wait outside, while he went in and secured the merchandise, me being barred from that kind of enterprise, since I'd emerged with two Mars bars - again! But fair play to Jimmy, he hadn't been that annoyed, maybe, because I'd included in my apologies how remarkably old he looked for his age. And, I assumed, buoyed by that knowledge, afterwards, he could go in and get served practically anywhere, although it was usually the same place. He'd even take off his helmet so as not to frighten the staff.

We'd carry our load then, mostly flagons of cider, we seldom bothered with anything else, in the bike's top-box, and under my arms; people like Rayo would often order too, up to Conroy's, where Jimmy's father, lying in wait, would pretend to object, until we slipped him the brown paper bag with the naggin inside, that we'd always have got for him, and then he'd bid us enter with the warning that, "this," couldn't continue. Local opinion had it that he'd invite in "the Devil himself," if he'd thought to bring along a dram of good or, indeed, any sort of whiskey.

And so it was, that on this particular night when I knocked on his door it was opened by he who had been one of the last inhabitants of the Planet X, that tragic world devastated by a terrible pestilence, that had rendered it's victims mindlessly dispassionate, and who, facing the prospect of their own extinction, had flung themselves far and wide in search of other species to massacre, preferably with their bare swollen hands.

The skin stretched on it's scarred, block-shouldered head, and the snarling, thin-lipped ortifice below the twisted nose-bruise made to another move, when, from behind it, a second, almost identical one, got in first to flaunt it's command of the unfamiliar language:"Who the fuck is this wanker?" it said.

But I was glad that there were two of them; serving to impede each other in the rush to get at me, they only leaving off chewing on each other's forearms, to ask: "Who the fuck is he callin' a Siko?"

"No," I pleaded, "that's my name! I'm a mate of Jimmy's!"

"Who's Jimmy?" they demanded.

It should be mentioned here, that the neighbours had got it wrong: they hadn't quite got rid of Mickey and his friends and motorbikes. The friends still called, and he had more of them now than when he was alive. Whether it was to pay their respects, or just to hide themselves or the gear that they'd stolen, their was seldom a day that the remaining Conroys were left alone. And, in fairness to the visitors, if they stayed, they didn't do so without contributing generously to the household budget, and taking great care not to upset Patrick.

But these two really bothered me. I only hoped that there weren't more of them inside, having terminated the living moments of the rightful occupants. Although, usually in those cases, I knew that it was normal for the alien invaders to adopt the shells of their victims, and not these thick-ignorant hulks, so that I should be assuming now that I was in the presence of Patrick and Jimmy's father, if a little bit puzzled, perhaps, about an inconsistent lisp or Scottish accent.

I was wondering if the house wasn't filled with them; guzzling our cider, swinging out of the lightbulbs, and probably sexually excited too from leering at the metal beauties in Mickey's old motorcycle magazines that they'd discovered in the cupboard where Patrick had hidden them, and God knows what they'd done to him! But after telling them of who Jimmy was, they motioned me inside to where he, Jimmy, was seated in company with his father and, I suppose, I should have been expecting this, the Black Prince himself!

* * *

"Siko Robbie Polly Dinko Robbie Siko Dinko Siko Polly Siko Robbie Polly Dinko Jimmy Jimmy Robbie Jimmy Polly Jimmy Dinko Jimmy Jimmy Polly Siko Dinko Dinko Dinko Dinko Polly ... ," Jimmy's father did the introductions.

"Robbie!" had got rid of the moustache and the hair, and was years younger, as well, but otherwise he looked exactly the same, and he was still smoking too. And, of course, he'd had the gall to barely disguise his name. But was that not his prerogative: for wasn't he the King of Gall! The Prince of Hell and the King of Gall!

The King of Gall had the ace of spades. The King of Gall was playing poker and had the ace of spades and the ace of clubs, against Jimmy's poor father who'd only had a pair of queens. "I thought I might have pulled another one," he'd said.

Jimmy, only after coming downstairs, flinched, and said: "C'mon Siko, let's get in on this!" and so I had to sit down opposite he who's game it was, he who should never, ever, be played against, and so it went: My two threes were to be no better than worthless against his three twos; Jimmy's three fours useless against his four threes; Jimmy's father's queens fell again; my pair of eights were outwitted by his sevens; three sixes thrice stole the spoils.

But then sometimes he'd leave a pot to us, but when he went "dead" there wasn't enough evidence of anything having killed him. It was just that he might make us believe that all things were fair or equal. He didn't fool me; the master of deception had no regard for any such concepts, but I couldn't tell the others that!

I was the first one out, then Jimmy's father, not that he'd been "cleaned," he 'd just drank himself under the table – again! We adjusted our feet. Only Jimmy was left.

How could I stop him? How could I stop him going everything when he showed me his hand – his "Dead Man's Hand": His pairs of aces and eights. "A dead man's hand never loses," we always said. But we were wrong; the dead man had to meet the Prince.

"Don't worry," he said to Jimmy, when he wasn't able to match his bid, "if you lose you can owe me."

I would have paid it, if I had it! I would have ran and stolen it from Kate, or borrowed it from Anna, if I'd had time to! I could have got it from Rayo, who was around somewhere making up, with a couple of bits of woods and a bicycle chain, a pair of somethingchycoos, as seen in Bruce Lee's film, for hitting the skinheads with — he was already good at the shout - if I'd thought that he wasn't as broke as he said he was. But Rayo was straight up! He wasn't the type who hid their money in their socks with their cigarettes, whom you'd kick in the shins when you met, and embarrass into cashing out, whilst claiming that it wasn't theirs at all, but their sick grandmother's, who was going to die if they didn't get her her medicine with it on the way home.

Not that I went around kicking people in the shins; they might kick me back and harder, and maybe give me a few digs as well, but I had seen it done! What to do now? Jimmy's father had left some cash on the table when he went down, but it wasn't enough! Maybe he had some elsewhere? Would I try and revive him ... ? But then it was too late: Ronnie produced his house of knaves, and I could only defy him by giving him my "mess with me and you'll be sorry that you were ever born look," that I'd been practising in the mirror -It didn't even look that ridiculous once I'd narrowed my eyes another bit - but it didn't bother Ronnie, not at all; he just ignored it, and kept on counting the change.

An innocent bystander might never have suspected that he knew that I was on to his game; that I was his mortal enemy, in league with his ancient foe, and had vowed, at least to myself, to battle with him to the, sure to be, bitter end. But then the innocent bystander was now in his power, and presuming that he'd meant everyone bar his father, I too complied with Ronnie's command, and followed Jimmy out to the van.

* * *

Patrick didn't come along. In fact, he didn't seem that interested at all in exacting revenge. I hadn't seen him that night, not even when we were leaving, which, though, might have been just as well, because he could have gone all sarcastic on us, in spite of what we were going to do for him: asking what kind of time did we think we'd be back, and did we want him to wait up, maybe to nurse our wounds, or to put on a hot-wash to rid our clothes of the bloodstains; he did that before for me. But he didn't as much as come down to wave us off, not that the Black Prince hadn't closed the door very gently behind him.

In the back of the van: an empty, dark, Ford Transitty thing, I thought about how we might get out of it. I must have been thinking with my lips moving, because Rayo asked me what I'd said. I answered, "nothing," but felt the worse for it, because for him and Jimmy, lost already, in their innocence, thought not that they were on the road to Hell, but merely off to do battle with Roly and the skinhead hordes. But, how could I tell them? What could I do? I had no ideas, and certainly wasn't inviting any in with the amount of nicotine and alcohol I was still consuming; both being found responsible for the wanton destruction of trillions of innocent brain cells, to be charged and convicted, and sentenced to a terrible future of social ostracism.

Ganged together as a vaporous stream they were, right now, flowing over my own little organisms, which, for some reason, looked to me like small grey mushroomy things, but with eyes and noses, drowning, choking, the lives out of them by the thousands, so that, and this was only calculating from the base of my present intake, which would surely quadruple by the six months, when I was eighteen, if I lived that long, I wouldn't have any left at all.

I could here them screaming: "Scree," they went. "Scree, Scree," and "Scree," again. No, I couldn't! It was just the van taking a corner, but I wondered about what it might be like to have none.

I looked at Dinko or Polly, whichever one of them it was, sitting on the floor across from me, who'd probably been born without very many, and I thought about Cocky O' Cleary, who'd probably gotten rid of most of his in the same way as I was now doing. He was back in the news again: Not satisfied, it seemed, with just following young schoolgirls, he'd taken now to doing "lewd" things in front of them, or so said Kate's sister Bridgit, who, personally, I figured, was just bitter because no one wanted to do lewd things for her anymore.

In truth, I hadn't figured it out by myself, I'd heard Anna saying it to Kate - you could now, she might even laugh! Anna was always a friend to Cocky, and not in the way of Agnes, who'd only been interested in his lewd things. Agnes brain cells had been diseased, her mushrooms had runny noses, which, though, didn't excuse her from anything. It was only when you had no brain cells that you could do whatever you liked. I took another swig from my flagon.

It was my second and last, but I'd made sure to let everyone know about the half bottle of vodka that I'd "skulled" beforehand. I was actually quite good at drinking; I'd shown a surprising natural ability. Already, I was almost up there with Jimmy, who'd been able to get in a lot more practice. I rarely puked, and I'd never poured it out whilst pretending to be pissing, the kind of underhand tactic that was usually reserved for the fields or parks, but I'd even seen it done into Conroy's sink, when Patrick wasn't around.

But then Polly's or Dinko's, whichever one of them it was, remaining behavioural monitors mustered together to seek their further annihilation, by having him say: "Hey John, gis a mouthful o' that, will ye?"

Now, I could have claimed that I'd have said it anyway, even if Jimmy or Rayo weren't sitting on either side of me, because I'd only a drop left and was already showing signs of getting pretty mean like that: "Me name's not John!" was what I'd replied.

"Give us over that fuckin' flagon," the cells demanded, "or I'll tear yer head off yer bleedin' shoulders!"

"Fuck off and buy your own!' was out before I knew it was coming, and I wouldn't have said that even with an army of Rayos and Jimmys beside me! But then I hadn't said it, I realised, I'd only been thinking it, but somehow, "whichever one of them it was," had read my mind. It must have been the Black Prince's influence! And, of course, Jimmy being in his power, and Rayo, rooting in his trousers for his whateveryoucallthem-chycoos, were slow in getting around to helping me. But, as I described earlier, I was experienced in this kind of situation, and was down before he even hit me. It wasn't that bad when you knew how to take it!

There were worse things; like going up for the ball, and instead of guiding it "majestically," or even, "spectacularly," into the "bulging net," it connected not with your forehead, or "forred', as it was only acceptably pronounced, but hit you on the back of the neck, and sent you sprawling down onto the road, where your hands might get cut and your knees could be torn, as well, and everyone would laugh, although there were people who laughed when I was getting a hiding too! Or, when a teacher crept up from behind and smacked you "around the earhole," because then you weren't prepared. I'd even been knocked out a few times, but, unfortunately, never in school, and it was fairly okay; my not knowing much about it afterwards.

But I did know a lot about it now, and it wasn't very pleasant, especially the hair pulling. I didn't really mind the the dull thuds on the side of the head. "The Dull Thuds," that sounded like a great name for a band! I tried to think about speaking to Herbert about them, but they wouldn't let me; they weren't showing any signs of letting up. I presumed that Rayo, and Jimmy, maybe too, were locked in mortal, if it's correct to say that here, combat with, "whichever one of them it wasn't," and possibly Ronnie, the driver, as well: The van was still moving, but surely that would be a deed of little consequence to him!

But then I was free, and I could see, although it was all a little bit blurred at first, but after a while, that I'd been wrong! The front two were still where they'd been, and Jimmy and Rayo were, singularly, involved with my man. Rayo swung from his neck, whereas Jimmy had his head stuck into his stomach, in a way that you couldn't tell who was winning. It was all very worrying, especially when "whichever one of them it wasn't," did climb into the back, and I hit the floor again.

Mercifully though, instead of the lads, he turned on his twin, identifying him: "Dinko! I've had enough of your shit!" And the van stopping now, he opened the door and pushed him out. He, Dinko, protesting wildly that it wasn't his fault, but the "ugly, little fucker's," who had started it. Still, I couldn't help but feel a bit sorry for him: imagine if Jimmy had done the same thing to me! Even if I was bound to shout, when he was safely exiled: "Go way ye big thick bastard. If I ever see ye 'round again I'll beat the livin' shite out of ye." But that was all very well, until "Polly" told me that I had to go too.

I would never again question Jimmy's loyalty, no matter who's spell he was under, because he pleaded for me to stay, claiming that I couldn't help being "the way that I was," and that I was neither "the full shillin,' nor "playin' with the full deck," that "the lights were on, but there was no one at home", and that "the lift wasn't goin' to the top floor", and if I threw in a load of "buts" myself, it was all to no avail.

Polly after grabbing my wrist and pushing it, painfully, up my back, in the manner popularised by the police – or the "Pigs," or the "Filth," as they were fashionably known – who did it to everyone, including their wives, girlfriends and children if they had any too, when they wouldn't do what they wanted them to, threw me out and left me, as the van drove away, sprawled on the road once more, looking up at Dinko, who wasn't laughing!

* * *

I hadn't a lot to go on in the way of peace offerings, having been, again as mentioned earlier, already divested of my Wrangler jacket, and if during the melee I'd protected the remains of my flagon by squeezing it tightly between my thighs (I'd obviously felt it was worth the risk!), it was all to no avail, because Polly wouldn't let me out of doors with it. But even with an off-licence full of the stuff, I doubted if it would have pacified Dinko. I waited for the worst, not having had the "neck" to "leg" it: I might have antagonised him further, and he'd catch me, I knew he would! That is assuming that Dinko and his kind knew varying degrees of antagonism. I supposed so, they not able in any other way to be.

It was rough for them, although those who handled it best could get jobs in films, especially old ones, where they'd put more scars on their faces and pay them for being cruel and viscous all the way to their grisly ends, brought about by falls from very tall buildings, crushings beneath runaway trains, stampings by horses with the proper attitude, dismemberments by the threshing of farm machinery, or, more times than not, mowings down by the combined forces of justice and order who, seemingly existing, thought all the more of themselves afterwards, and delighted their girlfriends too.

I was reminded of a film now, when on offering him a cigarette he grabbed the whole packet, but instead of beating me up again, said: "A skinny fucker like you might be useful." It featured: "Pip the Magic Dragon, who lived by the sea and was sent home by an escaped convict to get some gear for his tea." No it didn't! Or, at least, I made that up myself, an account of my being in the room alone when it was on television, and they having forced us to sing "Puff the Magic Dragon ..." in school not long before, and Pip in the film did have a very high pitched voice! Well, I'm sure you can understand where my confusion arose.

But it didn't come as any surprise to me, Pip meeting up with an escaped convict; after all he was hanging around a desolate graveyard, what did he expect! And, of course, there was no doubting that it was an escaped convict that he was dealing with; not with his clothes with the arrows on, and, if I remember correctly, he even had a bit of his ball and chain still attached (I mean.. come on..who writes that shite?). It really was a very disappointing film, because you always knew too that nothing very bad was going to happen to Pip: with his good manners and posh accent, things would be sure to turn out alright for him. But not for the likes of Dinko or the escaped convict, even if he did betray his character at the end.

Anyway, I had no great expectations now that Dinko was merely going to send me home for a sliced pan and a few slices of corned beef, or any other victuals, especially as to wherever it was I was going, he was coming too. I tried to delay my fate by mixing the blood from my nose and mouth together, then slurping it around and spitting it out onto the pavement, while exaggerating my limp at the same time. But Dinko didn't accept that I wasn't fit for duty, he gave me a kick "up the arse" and ordered me to move a lot faster.

But it could have been worse: I knew what it was that he had in mind for me. For, as he'd suggested, there was always a place for the "skinny fucker" in the land of the separated house.

* * *

Theirs was to sneak down laneways, climb walls, and stand with their legs wobbling and their stomachs churning, because not of the alcohol, until they were led up the garden path by non-skinny fuckers, with broader accents too, who released their ears only to properly alert them to the perils of barely opened windows atop downstairs sills, and implored, nay commanded, them to do or die: "Get up to that window, ye little cunt, or I'll tear off your ugly head and shit in the hole where it used to be!" Commander Dinko repeated his order of the laneway, before his troops had poured over the garden wall. "I'll tear off your balls and stuff them in your mouth! I'll play marbles with your eyes! I'll run your fingers through my hair ..."

Suitably encouraged, his men successfully mounted the sill. Not being a crack unit, however, they needed a period of recuperation before tackling their next objective. Then, although encountering heavy resistance in the form of, embarrassingly, uncoordinated footwork, they, eventually, managed to reach, through the gap, the handle of the bigger, lower pane. But again, belonging to a misfits outfit, and not being very bright either, they choose to retreat momentarily, only to land on their arses in the garden.

The Commander, a wily veteran, allowed them to fall, before exhorting them to pick themselves up again and renew their assault with increased determination, his cries of "Fuckin' eejit!" and "Tear your throat out!" ringing in their ears.

An insubordinate subordinate asking if he was to accompany them, he replied: "Me bollocks!" and motioned through to the main entrance, where they with him should rendezvous after he'd completed his own, outflanking, manoeuvres, then punched the back of their knees, causing them to disappear into the darkness.

They hadn't disappeared very far though, when they encountered a hostile sink unit that, if unable to halt the advance indefinitely, seriously dented it's moral, and other bits possibly too, and then, even if overrun, continued to harass the intruders by spraying a hail of drying delph after them, as they continued downwards to meet up with a harder foe:the floor.

Battered again in this fracas, and convinced that all enemy units must surely be alerted to their presence, what was left of the invading army made ready the white flag, but were surprised when no enemy officer emerged to take it. "But," the men thought, "It's too quiet. We don't like it when it's this quiet. It makes us nervous! It makes us scared! It causes us to break wind and think about bodily functions!" But then they did hear something! Or did they?

They decided that it must be a cat or the breeze or something. Not that that wasn't what they told themselves when they were at home in bed and thought that they'd heard a noise downstairs: That it was just, "a cat or the breeze or something," but they doubted that the enemy could be as lazy, or cowardly, or both. But no one appeared! So with a measure of courage restored, and contemplating once more the admonishments of their superior, they made haste to complete their mission.

Surprisingly, smoothly, ran things: They finding a door at the far end of the kitchen, pulled it back to be rewarded by the street-light glaring through the hall-door panes. But only until, when releasing a latch, the door still refused to budge. Not that they panicked, not even after again hearing the breeze or a cat or something, confident as they were that the door was fitted with one of those built-in mortice lock things, as seen recently in the home of their Aunt Kate, courtesy of their cousin Anna.

"Just have to find the key," they said. But searching, then frantically, they happened upon a small table that, upending itself defiantly, had left them scrambling about the carpet after it's escaping cargo, when they sensed the presence above them.

They considered warning it of the stronger force outside, as in: "There's a fella waitin' for me, and he's a mad bastard," but were settling for, "Please mister, he made me do it," only to be saved from doing so by the presence announcing itself: "You shouldn't", it said, "be here in the house of my father."

And they were okay then, because they realised that it was Herbert!

* * *

I should have recognised it: I should have realised that I was in Joseph's house! But what a diabolical thing for the forces of evil to do! But, what else should I expect! Was I that stupid? Was I that thick? Could I have actually believed that the Prince of Darkness was incapable of sinking so low; arranging for the half-brother of the Son of God to be party to the desecration of the house of the man who'd appeared to be his father? I think not!

"What are you doing in my father's house?" Herbert asked, again in his disguised voice. Apart from anything else, I'll have to say, he had a great sense of humour. But then weren't we all cast in his likeness, or, was it he in ours? But, anyway, I let him know that I got the joke: "Ha Ha Ha" I laughed, and "Ha Ha Ha" again, when he didn't respond.

But then, when he asked the same question again, I decided I'd play along. From the first stair I began, supposing that he might be also trying to get a line on my comprehension: "I'm here," I said, "at the behest of the Devil himself, to assist in the rape of this the house of your bastard father, whilst he drives my friends to Hell. "But," I added, "whatever should occur my lord, please forgive them for they knowest not what they do." I reckoned he'd appreciate that, especially the "knowest" bit, it sounding very biblical. "My brother, my lord, help me to help save them." The soft carpet beneath me as I moved slowly upwards felt exactly the same as before; how could I not have remembered! "My brother, my lord, my master, give me the wherewithal to be truly thy humble ally. Allow me to joust equitably with the Prince and his minions. Give me the strength to break their skulls. Give me the gift of tongues, soest I can tear their's out." But he was gone! Where was he?

On the landing now, I detected a movement in the nearest bedroom; the room of the liar Marian, who'd had no cat! But what an appropriate arena to begin the sacred fight against the dark forces; the she-devil had existed only to drain the soul from the good Joseph. Although, credit where it's due, the Black Prince, in sacrificing Agnes, had prevented another one developing.

Entering the room, I could see, with my mind's eye, the rose-patterned wallpaper from the magazines that Agnes would have looked at. And through, what would surely have been, the large bay-window, I pictured the daylight streaming around her white-smiling neighbours, tending their fanatically manicured sensible cars and gardens. This is what the bitch would have lived for!

But where was Herbert? From behind the door, I could hear him breathing! I slammed it shut, and, dropping to my knees, joined my hands together, and prayed: "Praise the Lord and death to the evil ones. Praise the Lord and death to the evil ones," I shouted then, and again and again.

Through the darkness waved he an instrument about me - It could have been a sword, but was more likely a poker – and sent me forth to pursue the good fight.

* * *

It had been a rough night, I'll have to admit. But I didn't mind, not now that I was going to get a look at Hell; I mightn't get the opportunity again. I mean, it wouldn't necessarily be a preview, with the connections I had, I was probably bound for elsewhere, especially if I acquitted myself well here. And I wasn't dead! Even if I had taken a heavy whack, I doubted that it had been fatal, me being expert ... I don't want to get into all that again!

So it was, that I tumbled backwards heels over head, and then head over heels, in a way that I'd often feared that I would: When sitting on a highish wall, I'd hunch forwards, as if that was how I always smoked my cigarettes, whereas others, like Jimmy, for instance, could lean back, same as they did when in the pictures, or having their tea or something, or hop along the top of it, with a makey- up limp, maybe, before grabbing me, and shouting: "Got chaa!" so that I'd have to try and disguise my heart attack, by saying: "Fuck off you bastard," and smiling, as if I wasn't at all bothered. Thankfully, that was happening less as we got older.

But I wasn't frightened now. In fact, I felt like the fellow who did it every week on our old television set when I was younger: I could see him, in his polo-neck jumper and stupid-looking hair style, swirling through a whirling mass of greys. I couldn't remember how it happened, whether he organised it himself, or it just came upon him when he was minding his own business, or doing other mundane things, but having got back to the year 860 BC, or whenever, he'd refuse to leave it again, until, not only had he sorted out the current problems, but prevented more occurring by teaching the kids back then to respect to their elders, and other peoples property too. And if they were wealthy kids, to pay proper attention to their studies, as well. Or, was I confusing it with another programme? Or, had there been a programme at all?

My colours now weren't grey, but strongly black and white. Black in the main, white in the bits that reminded me of the people in the photographic negatives that you weren't supposed to touch (Jimmy and his father were forever amused to see each other that way!). Yet if I was dead, and my soul, or I, was floating aimlessly through the infinite blackness of the universe - the white bits being stars, or pure things on their way to Heaven, perhaps? - then I was happy, not being told what, or having anything else, to do, and even careless about football, or music, or films that I might have seen, or, as much as, Jimmy and girls that I might have fancied.

But then my fall ended and, like any other traveller who arrives, I had to leave my craft, or, in my case, get off my knees, to appreciate where I'd come to, to be able to tell, to anyone who would listen, that I'd set down in a dying world, where I would surely perish unless I could summon from my exhausted being the strength to strike for the mountain range, taking along the way nourishment from the mysterious underground stream that would, doubtlessly, spring from it.

The mountain range of this particular world, however, tempted not the weary traveller, for he was denied their promises by the high window-barred walls, where crept through only the moon's beam alighting on to the piled crates and bottles and the stone staircase that climbed up to the, sure to be, locked cellar door. So, dusting himself down, he waited for the hunchback to arrive.

* * *

I had a fear of rats too, and with very good cause. That is to say, although I didn't hate them because of my fear, if they hated me I fully understood.

Jimmy and I used to go 'rattin," which was exactly as it sounded. The venue was a neglected site where an old building had been demolished. We'd get in amongst the rubble, and the rubbish that had been dumped on top of it, and kick about until a rat would appear. We'd chase it then and bombard it with our armfuls of stones, causing it to disappear, or, oftentimes, disappear squealing, because we had our hits, especially Jimmy, of course. But, as we never found any corpses, I'd always wondered what had become of those dying rats.

Alhough Jimmy would claim, modestly, that we'd only "winged" them, I was never convinced. I'd decided that they'd died as they like to live: hidden away from the eyes of humankind. But I'd been wrong! They'd gone straight to Hell, body and soul, and were in my cellar now. I could hear the patter-pit of their damaged feet! Never again, I swore, would I harm a hair on the head of another creature (that covered me for the hairless ones!), living or dead, if I survived this. But then their movements stopped, and they were standing on their hind legs in the shadows leering at me.

I tried to see them differently: I took away their superior smiles and their black eye-patches; I put heavy coats on their bleeding emaciated bodies; I transmogrified them through the white mouse-gerbil-hamster spectrum; I had them eating cabbage leaves and jogging brainlessly on treadmills; I tried to forget that they ate not just their own but other's young too, that they carried vile diseases and were responsible for the willful destruction of grain stocks, that they chewed their way through power cables and various non-perishable materials, thereby being a blight on industry as well as agriculture and a threat to the working man....there wasn't a good word to be heard about them in school. And then there were the 'exposed throat' stories – what a curse it was to be marginalised!

But, so it was, that, again, I pictured their snarling fangs dripping saliva, and there slender whiplash tails beating impatiently, like a cat's would do(?), anxious for the kill. Then, back on all fours, they were crawling towards me. Weakly, my shivering legs carried me up the steps, my feeble palms patted on the wooden door, "Help! Help!" I shrilled.

"Who's there?" enquired the hunchback.

* * *

"Who is it? Who's there?" asked the hunchback again.

"It's only me," I said. "Billy ... Billy Sikes!"

"Billy Sikes!" said the hunchback, "How come I know that name?"

"In a book," I said, "you probably came across it in a book." The rats were at the foot of the steps.

"I doubt it," said the hunchback, "I never bothered with many."

"Well then the film,"I said, "you probably saw the film." The rats were on the middle steps.

"Maybe," said the hunchback, "but I can't say that I remember it. Tell me, what was it called?"

"The Revenge of the Stoned Rats," I shouted, they were pissing against my leg now! "Will you open the fuckin' door!"

"Certainly," replied the hunchback, in time-honoured fashion, "why didn't you ask before?"

"Of course," he said, after he'd dragged back the bolts and I'd leapt through the gap, "I mightn't have seen it at all, it's more likely the effects of collective consciousness."

"What are you shiting about?" I said, now strangely comfortable in the darkness.

"Oh don't mind me," said the hunchback, "it's just amazing what you get to thinking about when you're on your own, and without the emotional distractions of live and love. But," he said, "not everyone can be the Keeper of the Gates of Hell."

"I suppose so," I agreed then, surprisingly, "most everyone has heard of Bill Sikes somehow, and him just a character in fiction, like Robin Hood and the Hound of the Baskervilles."

"That's where you're wrong," the Hunchback dissented, "Bill Sikes is every bit as real to me as you are now Billy Sikes, but then," he said, "I am full of shite, you'd only have to ask anyone who ever knew me."

We moving, I'd followed his voice until the scene changed,

becoming quiet in the blazing brightness. The flaming wall torches glaring, shockingly, down on us, we glanced at each other, shyly, and turned away again. I'd seen a lot!

He wasn't really a hunchback, not technically, I suppose, that you'd see, maybe, in the late night 'Hammer Horror' films, but he did stoop small and bow-legged, and he was dressed in traditional hunchback gear: medieval-style hooded jerkin, boots and clothed tights. And his face, before he'd raised the hood, was the usual pock-marked ulceration, broken only by a squashed-looking nose, and a couple of black teeth peeking out from behind a pair of weeping lips, his hairs just slimy bits slithering down his oily neck.

"Will waa di ye expec?" he slurred, self-consciously.

"Oog coos mae," I'd blushed in reply, always susceptible to that kind of influence.

We travelled on, and down and down again, the passageways' falling flights of steps.

"Ma yor hid!" he warned in the light. I ducking, was forced first to adopt the demeanour of the hunchback, and then to drop to my hands and knees, as the ceilings got lower and lower. The walls closing in too, and there being no one around who knew me, I screamed in panic: "Get me out of here! Please, get me out of here!"

But, "Not much further," the hunchback drooled, in the then relative darkness.

He spoke the truth, and I could stand again when at another door the hunchback knocked.

"Who's there?" a voice boomed from the other side.

"Anto," said the hunchback, "Anto and young Billy Sikes."

"Billy Sikes!" said the someone from beyond, "how come I've heard of him?"

Not that I was surprised to find that I'd been keeping

company with the Devil's favourite advocate; although Anto was even more the "little runt" than Ronnie would have had me expect him to be, if, in fairness, being run over by Mary's jeep hadn't helped his cause. But still, she'd been willing to bestow on him her favours, which went to show that there was hope for us all!

We were invited over the threshold. "Meet and match," the hunchback said, slipping away from my side, the invisible voice not even staying that long.

The room was illuminated, but only by the glowing cigarette tips of it's occupants and the strange scarlet sheen emanating from the glassy floor beneath us. I turned to see two leather clad men crossing tongues passionately, the three skinheads beside them, showing no heed, continued to "Fuck this," and "Fuck that," conversationally. A wide-legged woman stood over what appeared to be the source of the glow, nearly naked from the waist down, her hands crept down to her crotchless knickers, causing me to feel the same way - well it wasn't the queers, or Bambi being mounted by the Hound of the Baskervilles further along the wall!

But then a callow youth took me by the shoulder, and begged me join him in an ale.

* * *

A bar had conveniently appeared from the shade of the far-facing wall, a replica of one I was familiar with from our rare visits into town Although, it seemed not to accommodate the baldy-headed barman who'd refused to serve us after enquiring of our ages, on the mathematical grounds of nineteen, if greater than eighteen, was still a way short of twenty-one. That chastening experience, well for Jimmy anyway, I imagined, had left us, though, all the wiser, and from there on we'd sit in a far corner and let someone who was really over eighteen, if not twenty-one, go up and get our drinks for us. Even if people of that vintage were thin on the ground of that establishment, most of them, like Mickey, when Jimmy had talked him into coming along with us, when furnished with a drink, demonstrated their maturity by classifying it as "piss-water," and walking out, vowing never to return again. Anyway, we had much better fun drinking out of doors, or up in Conroy's.

As their wasn't a barman evident now, hairless or otherwise, my new companion went behind to fill the drinks himself. If about the same age and height as myself, he appeared to me to be even scrawnier, so that structurally he reminded me of a five o' clock chicken: On a Sunday, after the sumptuous bits have been devoured, and all that remains would make a good dog choke, or so they said; Agnes trying it on the neighbours hadn't had any success, that particular mongrel also being too wise for her.

He faded even further then, before re-emerging with two tankards of a foaming brew that looked to be, at least, a god's piss, and likely to put hair on both his and my bones. But, gulping a mouthful, I was disappointed to become no Mr. Hyde, if well compensated by it tasting the same as the very concoction I'd been deprived of earlier: It was cider with a head! I mentioned the fact.

"Yes," he said, "you get what you like down here ... mine's a schnapps!"

After three more of them he told me his life story.

Born into a prosperous town, he was the son of a master carpenter, and, as he said himself: "My sisters and I knew a comfortable childhood, when I'd finished my schooling I should learn the skills and, having first found a wife, take over the reins of his thriving business from my aged father."

"But," he said, "when still not much more than a boy, I was overtaken by demons. Demons who came to me in the guise of aloneness and hopelessness. I had questioned my very reason for being, and receiving no answer, decided that I was but the merest blot on the copybook of existence. Everything then to me, became no better than worthless."

"I fell out with my father, my sisters, my mother, my schoolwork suffered, the few friends I'd had were left behind, it being impossible for me to consider them; my feeling of aloneness making them no more than playthings of my imagination, my own consciousness the disturbed product of some cruel god's joke."

"Trying to find a measure of relief in the pounding pavement, I walked the town every night, my journeys often culminating in the ruins of it's ancient and neglected castle. Climbing to the battlements, I'd consider throwing myself therefrom, but saw no guarantee of escape that way; the boundaries of so called life and death to me being indeterminately blurred. But, I have to say, the castle did grant me a certain solace, a feeling, perhaps, of a history that was real."

"But then, as suddenly as they'd arrived, the demons departed, leaving me with an appreciation of being that I'd never known before. However, filled with this new verve, instead of settling, I intensified my rebellion against both work and play, was expelled from my school for my constant displays of indiscipline, and forbidden by my father to leave the house in the evenings, in his attempt to thwart my growing association with the local delinquents. Not that I didn't anyway, in spite of his beatings!"

"But," he said, "in time I quietened. I was found another

school, the concern of a harsher regime, and even if there was no appreciable improvement in my schoolwork, I was given less scope for my misdoings. Also, I had grown tired of the destructive ways of my companions and had taken to my solitary ramblings again, if with a lighter step than before. Oftentimes, returning to the castle, where from it's battlements I would gaze down restlessly at my easily contented world, and it's all pervading order. Wistfully, I would recall the battle cries of the warriors of old who, in deference to their masters, fired their crude weapons at his enemies. I heard the screams as the arrows bit and the oil scalded, but meditating on the horrors of those cruel ages, I still considered them preferable to the middling predictabilities of my modern living."

"Then came the first occasion when I felt that I was being observed, but was unable to detect another visitor to the dilapidating castle. Journeying homeward, I felt that eye still upon me, and hearing a footfall behind, I turned to see but a still deserted street. Blaming it on a cat or the breeze or something, I tried to put it from my mind, but couldn't when everywhere I went now, it was the same."

"The spectre terrified me, rousing as it did the ghosts of my black past. I became confused and deeply pensive once more, my sense of reality impinged upon again. In an effort to elude it, I took, to the delight of my parents, to staying at home in the evenings, and for the sake of being in company, whence it seemed to leave me, to juggling my schoolmates so as to always have one who would accompany me to it, reliably."

"Strictly adhering to this discipline, came the day when the unseen eye became just another bad memory from my dark stages, so much so, that I chose to throw away my weary rules and schedules and forsake my dull companions. And one morning, after making haste to avoid being apprehended by the calling scholars, and leaving behind the excuse of preparing work for classes, I set out again for the castle, but was strangely relieved, if truth be told, to become aware of a following behind me. It was in the ruins that he showed himself."

"I knew who he was! It was in the remains of what was once a grand banqueting hall, where he stood, tall and dark, before me, reminding me of a time when he'd also wandered abroad. A, speechlessly, strange man, we children were warned clear of him: it being generally told of how he was guilty of committing the awfullest of obscure and unproven crimes, against not just the young, but their god and animals too. Being able to tolerate no more, the good citizens had banished him from our town."

"But here he was now, reaching into the brown paper bag that he had always carried, and saying: 'Take this my body! Take this my blood!' And, having feasted, I climbed with him back up to the crumbling battlements, where, at their weakest point, he said: 'Wilhelm, there is another world.' and pushed me clear."

"What was in the bag?" I asked.

"Brown bread and oranges," he replied.

* * *

I should have guessed! "You are what you eat," they were starting to say, and Herbert had been partial to his brown bread and oranges; Kate had kept a special supply in for him. Me? I was a thin white slice without the crust, but with plenty of butter on.

My fellow disciple and I were quiet now, watching the lady dance over the inferno. (Either that, or the light came from those coloured bulbs used in the coal-effect electric fires, that were popular in my day) From somewhere, she'd gotten hold of two pistols, and now, in a frenzy, shoved them, simultaneously, into her mouth and crotch before, disappointingly, prematurely (I thought so anyway!), pulling the triggers, to spread her entrails over and amongst us.

The room echoed with gore. I rubbed my eyes to see the hunchback in scarlet and the skinheads lustily wax their crowns, the leather twosome copulating frantically, in an ecstasy of sleaze.

"Women!" Wilhelm remarked.

I asked him exactly what he meant: "Huh?" I said.

"The anguished heroine syndrome," he relied, "they all suffer from it to some extent. It's been propagated through the ages by every popular medium: the theatre; the novel; the cinema; television, depending on what era you are coming from. It gives a woman a false sense of value in the scheme of things, making believe a world revolves around her, and that, out there somewhere, there's a prince waiting to cure all her ills. It's the game they play," he said, "the illusion they create."

Wiping more of the illusion from my brow, I asked him if men didn't do the same thing.

"Yes," he said, "but outlaws are less lethal. At it's worst," he said, "the women affected can make theirs and everyone else's lives around them a misery. They can make themselves fat and ugly. They can pull the arms of their favourite dollies. (Agnes again!) They can even instigate their own killings at the hands of family members."

"Pray tell!" I pleaded.

* * *

"I was besotted once," he said, "with a friend of my sisters, a dreamy eyed young miss called Anika."

"It so happened, though, that Ingrid, the sister that she was friendly with, was the one that I liked the least. A selfish, cruel girl she'd made life as difficult as she could for me all through my early years. I couldn't tell what Anika saw in her, at all! When Anika visited and I tried to loiter, she would shoo me away: 'Shoo ...' she would say, just like that!"

"But given the slimmest of opportunities, and they came in plenty during the long school holidays, when the lazy Ingrid would refuse to rise from her bed to keep her appointments, I'd present myself to Anika, but struggled for words, and had only my anxious manners to make my feelings known."

"Alone in bed at night, I could, wistfully, discuss with her the subjects that would surely touch her soul, but, sadly, in practice, I failed to get past the weather, school and where she might be going with my hated sister that day. But, although I never received no more than the politest of replies, I took this as no indication of her not reciprocating my intent."

"So, believing that the hurriedness of our encounters in the home environment would never be conducive to our proper communication, and that the time had come to take her away from it, I decided to ask her out. But where to? I was too young to have money but ... we could walk together? What better! But, how to ask her?"

"The holidays were drawing to a close; I had no time to spare! I couldn't eat. I couldn't sleep: 'Would you ... ? Could you ... ? Will you ... ? Please ... ! Please ... ! Please ... !'"

"But then, at the eleventh hour, I finally found the strength, and standing stock stern before her, said: 'Anika, would you kindly join me in a walk tomorrow?'"

"Then I heard the laughter! Not from Anika – at first – but

from the doorway, where, unbeknownst to me, the drowsy Ingrid had been standing."

"'Ho Ho Ho,' she guffawed, like the moron that she was, 'Do you really believed that a girl like Anika would be bothered with an insect like you?' And poor Anika, only to cover her painful embarrassment, was forced to laugh then too. I staggered from the room, tripping and falling over a chair-leg on the way, to complete my agony."

"I stayed awake that night too, and for many more after, but the pain was gradually being eroded by the urge for vengeance. It was later, much later, and only after my terrible black period, that it was sated."

"I had devised a plan. My father, the carpenter, who had himself been responsible for the original construction of our house, and had later decided - it would have been his idea of a diversion - to add a wooden balcony to the rear of it, where, on a sunny day, whoever might desire, could place themselves under the gaze of the most affluent members of our society who dwelled on the hillside behind us. And so it was left neglected, except, of course, by the vain Ingrid. I chose to loosen the props of her stage."

"It was quite a simple task really, even for one such as I who, people said, showed no signs of having inherited the abilities of my father. I just had to loosen the appropriate stays and then wait for the sun to emerge again, into that dull summer, and tempt the bold Ingrid out."

"And it did, and she did, but the structure held fast! So I was bound for more nocturnal tamperings, wondering how much could really be required to support that fat frame? Until, finally came the day glorious to the deity's finest specifications; the sky shining blue, the sun burning bounteously from his heavens."

"Despondent now of my plot ever succeeding, I was in my room, amusing myself, when I heard the creaking. Dropping everything, I rushed out gleefully, but only in time to watch, in horror, as not just Ingrid, but the beautiful Anika too, fall screaming from the collapsing timber. Anika being far too modest to expose herself so, had obviously been intimidated by my ugly sister!"

"And Ingrid was fortunate; somehow she'd managed to throw herself sideways, and avoided the lines of straight-backed, sharpened stanchions, stored directly beneath the balcony and crucial to the formation of my plan. She'd hit the ground hard, and been killed almost instantly. Anika wasn't so charmed."

"Impaled on one of the stakes, it protruding grotesquely from her heaving bosom, bravely still, she spoke before she went: 'Wilhelm,' she said, 'what you did was true. It just would have been so much better if I hadn't to die too.'"

* * *

"The German killer awoke before dawn, he put his boots on;" the words of that well known ditty waltzed across my brain. Wilhelm arrived back with more refills. He being quiet now, I could think up a name for him: 'Just Wilhelm?' 'Wilhelm of Black?' 'Wilhelm Kill Them?'... I lost my train of thought: "And so how are you doin', yourself?" I asked a passing WANTON SLUT – she had it engraved across her forehead – but still, she passed on by! 'Little Wilhelm wont go home again?' Definitely not, that was embarrassing! 'Wilhelm the Psychotic?' 'Wilhelm Von Psychopath?' That was it! That was what I'd recall him as in the here on, if there was to be one!

Unjustifiably so, it was only because it would sound

interesting and dangerous. Like lots of other German killers, he'd had his reasons, good or bad. It was just a matter of getting beyond Captain Hurricanes's "Swinehunts," and appreciating the dehumanising aspects of the Eastern Front (I mentioned those paperbacks earlier.), and poor Wilhelm had had his in the shape of the vile Ingrid. Tragically, his breaking away from it had resulted in the casualty that he couldn't have envisaged. And, now here he was sitting in Hell, with but his favourite cup to console him – there was justice after all! Even if it had taken Herbert to see it done.

"So this is Hell!" I said, in my best sociable manner, to let him know that I didn't think any the worse of him, that, in fact, although I wondered if my best sociable manner was really up to it, I applauded his courage, and had cheered when the terrible Ingrid cracked her skulled, but, of course, sympathised painfully with the loss of his lovely Anika.

But he didn't show any signs of having heard me, so I screamed into his ear: "SO ... THIS ... IS ... HELL!"

Pushing himself up from the bar and his remembrances, and straightening himself once more on his stool, he replied:

"No it isn't!"

"But," I said, "I'm supposed to be in Hell!"

Removing my hands from his throat, he said: "Relax ... will you! It isn't Hell, but it's Paradise, and from here there's easy access."

"Show me!" I implored.

"Stay for a while," he replied, "have another drink ... you'll get there! But if you really have to, join with the skinheads, they'll be on their way soon. There isn't many who can settle for Paradise.

"Yes," I said, "I must hurry."

"So be it!" he replied, and, "I wasn't able to do this until I came here ..." Reaching for his mouth, he inserted two fingers and whistled, in the way that I was sure that I still couldn't: "Wheeeo whiit," he called. The skinheads started to file across.

"Fuckin, Bleedin', Fuckin', Bleedin Fuckin' Bleedin'... " they marched there way over. Halting, they said: "Huuuh?" I returned that greeting. Anto, having been dragged over in their tow (Or by his, it might seem later!), at a signal from Wilhelm, turned the procession back to where we'd entered earlier.

I said: "See ya," and he, Wilhelm, answered: "Auf Wiedersehen!" "Mein Gott ist in Himmel!" and "Englander Pig Dogs!" The skinheads? They weren't, but foreigners often made that assumption.

Then Anto, properly the hunchback again, led us out to where he had with me stood before. Facing two more doors, and without any help from the other side, he pulled the nearest one wide and let us through. It slamming behind us, we hesitated, before a skinhead disentangled himself from the mass and brought us away.

* * *

Strung out along the highway, a juggernaut dazzled us with it's glaring lights. Bracing ourselves to stand steadily against it, it whoosed on past. Although, back in the twilit world then, that feeling of solidarity was quickly forgotten, the skinheads turning ugly. But the lead's one, "Gis a smoke John ..." routine, passed along to me at the back of the line, was curtailed by an explosion of light and noise that made believe that my head had been blown apart, and that I was again tumbling across a Universe, until I cleared my eyes, picked myself up and recognised that it had, in fact, been his! Blood spouted from the lying torso, a leg kicked alone, there was nothing much else left to comment upon.

The skinhead, who had been following immediately behind appeared unhurt, but burst into a shocked (?) laughter, "Look at the state of Ao," he said, "the silly cunt!" pointing at the mess. The third one was similarly affected, even making a bad joke about "His" and "Mine". I, myself, retched again, but only tokenly, perhaps, pleased to suspect that I too was becoming desensitised to that kind of violence.

The high-jinks continued: Co lamenting the fact that that "miserable swine, Ao" had owed him a fiver, Bo, discovering Ao's clenched fist, threw it at him, remarking that there was a "bunch a' dem" for him, and that he should "take it ouha' dat!". Further merriment was only averted when another juggernaut came screaming towards us and exploded spectacularly in the nearer distance.

We dropped to our knees, praying that no sort of flying object would descend upon us, and we escaped. But then, readying ourselves for the off again, Bo dictated that we should piss. Standing next to me, he said: "Hey bollocks face," shaking his own out, "d'ye think that they're really out there waitin' to get us?"

Screening my own with my own outstretched palm (thumb?), I said "Yes," and then, "Who?"

"Them," he said, "that's always been out to get us: "Pigs and screws, and social workers, and oul fellas with neat gardens and shiny cars, and bus inspectors with pianos and kids who are good in school, and hurley players and pensioners, and religious bastards of all denominations, and youth activities organisers, and priests and bouncers, and brainy bastards of all ages ..."

"Definitely," I said, before we moved on.

"C'mon then," Bo ordered, "let's get off the main road and make it all the harder for them to find us."

On the uneven, rougher ground now, we fell often, but we dropped to seek it's shelter too, the explosions continually surrounding us, to rise again and hear the sound of gunfire away in the distance. What fun was had by all!

* * *

Every episode of cowboys and indians I'd featured in, every war game I'd ever played, were preparation for this. Every race I'd run, every wall I'd climbed, every chase I'd gotten, was just practice for now. Every mask I'd worn, every shape I'd thrown, every self I'd pretended to be, was for examination here. How many got the opportunity?

I thought about those I'd known who were faster, fitter, stronger, braver than I could ever be; where was to be their testing ground? Or, would they, like Jimmy's father, perhaps, dwell their tragic forevers on the might have been. I thought about my good friend Jimmy, that natural leader of men, what of him? Already an apprentice something or other, someday, if he survived, doubtless he be somebody's chargehand, in some or other workshop. And of Mickey and the other knights of old, who didn't die so young, what of them? Or did they ever not!

I thought about school and it's sporting heroes, who were, and not in spite of their prowess, safely ensconced behind the desks of banks and building societies, at most, battling it out at weekends with the elemental forces that ruled the golf course. I thought about Joseph and his awful wife. I thought about courage, valour, strength, excitement, euphoria, depression, cruelty, exhilaration, tension, elation, anxiety, cowardice, weakness, apprehension, intimidation, devastation and other concepts not compatible with the domestic language. I thought about war and I thought about love too, and then, come the next explosion, I thought about nothing but survival!

Distinctly closer this one had been; the ground chewed up hot around me. There was no sign of my "mates." I rose, and called: "Bo, where are you? Co, are you okay?"

"Over here Siko!" (When I'd told them what to call me they'd accepted it immediately – and me as well, I think!)

It was Co; the one without the ear-ring. Seated in a shell(?)-hole, he clutched a damaged wrist, blood dripped from the torn leg of his Wranglers, but he seemed cheerful, for he snorted gleefully at the dirt beside him.

"Look," he said, "at what's been following!"

And there, indeed, with it's head buried in the muck, and it's little rump aimed toward the skies, was the distorted body of Anto: the hunchback.

"What's he doing here?" I asking, and so leaving myself exposed to Co's lightning wit.

"Not a lot!" he said, "Not a fuckin' lot, by the looks of things!" he repeated for the hard of hearing, and then snorted some more, before letting go of his side, and composing himself for the serious note. "A leopard doesn't change it's spots," he said, "same as a skinhead, no matter how much hair you put on him, will always be a skinhead beneath it."

He went on: "You can isolate him. You can put him in a cage. You can drug him with what's legally available. You can try to rehabilitate him, but," he said, "if he was genuine in the first place, you'll never change him. That's why this little bollocks had to come after us."

Silence, and more of it then, before I asked: "Where's Bo?"

"I think he's over there," Co said, pointing, "and there and there, and over there too, more than likely." He was a funny man but, unfortunately, his humour wasn't infectious; the hunchback moaned, to have Co kick him, and enquire as to, "What the fuck?" he was whinging about, and then again, with the rejoinder that he shouldn't look at him in that "tone of voice" – Anto, on top of all his other ailments, seemingly having had his eyes transferred to the back of his head.

Swinging once more with his good leg, Co's bad one let him down, landing him in a heap over his target. But, not discouraged, he struck Anto on the head again with his better fist, before aiming lower with his Doc Martin. Anto squealed.

"Leave him!" I implored, "What have you got against him? Isn't he one of yours?"

Co pondered on this a while, before answering: "He's a stumpy little fucker, that's what!"

I thought about stumpy little fuckers who I'd known.

* * *

"Make war on the stumpy little fucker," the god of the skinheads had decreed, "do onto him as thoust will: Hurt him, use him, let him feel your shame and know your rage. Hate him, but fear him too; for he is thine enemy, because no matter how low he appears to be, he is never as low as you."

Although, a bit of a stumpy little fucker herself, Agnes had actually killed one once, a live performing dwarf he'd been – really! We were all at a circus (Kate had known someone!), and a troupe of them were running around, throwing buckets of water over each other, falling of the backs of elephants and generally behaving as they were expected to, thereby keeping everyone happy, and even happier then, when Agnes, from her ringside seat (Kate had known someone very important!), shot stones at them from the gun that she'd, forcibly, removed from some local cowboy, that was, in actuality, only supposed to be used for firing wooden corks at "Mickey Mouse" hanging things (I know, because Roly Brophy had had one later!).

She kept it on her lap, underneath our programme, but then when they chased close by, she'd try to, from beneath the cover of the acrobat, tiger, cigarette pack and hair-polish pictures, zap them on the ears, necks or any other area of exposed flesh that she was attracted to. She had a good hit rate too. In fact, I'd have to concede, that she was a crack shot! Although, she wouldn't let anyone else try for comparison: she said that I'd only get caught, and that I was bound to miss, anyway.

Anna kept whispering to her to stop: she wouldn't inform, that wasn't her style! But, even still, I was sure I'd heard her sniggering too when a dwarf was "plugged" and then stopped to wince with pain, whilst looking towards us suspiciously. But it was just one of those times when you couldn't help yourself – no matter who you were! And we were all so young, so very young. Although, Agnes would have always found it funny, no matter what age she might have gotten to; Agnes would have, forever, laughed at someone falling from a chair; Agnes would have, forever, pulled the chair from beneath them.

The rest of the kids, and even Kate, were enjoying it as well, until it took a turn for the serious, or the better, depending where you saw it from: A fast-passing dwarf suddenly grasped his throat and fell to the ground, his little body jerking wildly. Of course, we were all "in knots" with the laughing, especially when another one, having crouched down to examine his mate, started screaming: "A doctor? Is there a doctor in the house?"

I mean we were really "coiled up," until the lower one stopped jerking, and the other one kept screaming, and we got bored then, and started booing and calling for the rest of the show. So, the ringmaster did take action, and ushered on, not an actual doctor, but two of those spotty-faced lads in the black and white uniforms, with the handbags, who usually stood around rugby pitches and gymkhanas at the weekends, in an inappropriate response to the prospect of the sons and daughters of the rich getting hurt.

I supposed, they were looking even more embarrassed than they usually did, in the clothes that their mammies made them wear, and they unsure of what they should be doing; not being convinced that the dwarves weren't still performing, and that they might be about to become the butt of a bigger joke. And it was in butts, and the uniforms that their mammies made them wear, that Agnes saw her opportunity.

Bent down above her earlier victim, mumbling – I imagined that they might be arguing about who would give him the kiss of life; he being so ugly! - the heavier of them had exposed, for the interested eye, the upper end of his buttocks anatomy, and Agnes, taking aim, seemed to strike in the cleft between them. He howled and jumped to his feet, and, unselfconsciously now, massaged the stricken part. We all howling too, the poor dwarf was dumped on to their stretcher and ran from the arena. What a show!

The rest of the dwarves didn't reappear that night either, being replaced by some performing seals who were nothing like as funny. Agnes took aim again, but Anna, grabbing the gun from her, told her that: "Enough was enough!" So the seals were left unmolested, at least by the audience.

Curious to know the fate of the struck-down dwarf, the following day, I asked Kate about it, but she answering: "You know as much as I do," led me to my room where, lying on my bed, I couldn't come up with much more than the names and jerseys colours of several football teams, most of my nine times tables, and the realisation that Patrick, Jimmy's brother, was one of those spotty-faced lads with the handbags.

He hadn't been there himself that night, he told me, being away helping an auntie, he said (His mammy having run off with the milkman even before then; Patrick wore the uniform with pride!). Neither, he said, had he heard anything, but that he'd make enquiries and let me know as soon as he did. And, true enough, next time he called he had the information with him.

Arriving in full regalia, he sparkled from the peak of his policeman's-like hat to the tips of his periwinkle shoes. Then, after hanging his bag with the band-aids and the Marietta biscuits (I'd sneaked a look into it before, and a couple of the Mariettas!) at the foot of the stairs, he went in to talk to Anna.

I following, sat down at the kitchen table beside him and his polished buttons (He'd never understood that Anna wasn't impressed by that sort of thing!) until, after a while, Anna, graciously, enquired if there was anything that they could assist me with: "Can we help you?" was what she said.

So, regretfully, refusing to spare the ears of her young womanhood, I just asked: "Is he dead?"
And Patrick was straight: "Yes," he answered, "he is."

So, with that, I stormed up the stairs, and burst into the room where Agnes was busy dismembering another one of her dollies, and demanded that I had to talk to her: "NOW!"

But she leapt up from the floor, grabbed me by the ear, and said: "DON'T YOU EVER DO THAT AGAIN!" And refused to let me go until I said that I was sorry, and that I was sure that I was sorry, and that I was sure that I was sure that I was sorry "O Great One," only then could I run away and shout back: "You killed that poor performing dwarf, you mean person you," I really was very young and very innocent back then!

Of course, Agnes was never either: "Get out of my fuckin' sight you pathetic little prick you, I've had enough of your poxy drivel. Everyone knows that the short-arsed wanker had a heart attack. I never went near the bastard!" she screamed after me.

And she got away with it, but she was bound to: Anyone would have known that "they" were never going to conduct a full scale murder enquiry in to the death of a poor dwarf with a pebble stuck in his throat. They had much more rewarding things to do, and, anyway, the audience wouldn't have been that interested. Still, I couldn't have considered it very important myself, because I practically forgot all about it. But, it just went to show that Agnes had been a skinhead too!

* * *

Co was undergoing a crisis of conscience, teetering on the brink he was of betraying the mores of the late Bo, and probably Ao's too. "I'm getting nowhere," he was thinking, "I'm wondering aimlessly, and it's only a matter of time before they get me as well. At least on the highway there'd be the chance of making it to a city or town, or some sort of settlement – for could that be what I really wanted?"
Although, he didn't put it that way: "I've a pain in me arse," he said, "of crawlin' in and out of holes, let's get back to the fuckin' road!"

"What," I asked, "about the mines and the booby-traps?"

But he'd been undergoing an idea too: "No problem," he said, "we can shove the short-arsed wanker out in front."

"No," I disagreed, "the poor fella's not up to it, he wouldn't last pissin' time."

Co considered my second thought first: "Doesn't matter," he said, "he'll get us along some of the way, and then we can find a replacement." And my first thought second: "Don't mind all that moanin', he's just tryin' to smarm his way out of things. There's fuck all wrong with him! C'mon hunchback," he said, "stand up there and let's have a look at you."

Anto, trying to oblige, only managed some sort of facial press up.

"God he is ugly," Co observed, "How are ye supposed to tell when he's lookin' well or not?"

Anto about to collapse again, Co flicked him belly-up with his good Doc Martin, and then, squeezing it alongside the bad one on Anto's chest, said: "Well hunchback, what did ye want to go and mess me about like that for?"

"Velly solly," Anto apologised.

"What did he say?" Co asked me, starting to bounce now, "Is he bein' smart? Is he takin' the piss? Is he slaggin' me?"

"No! No! Don't!" I protested, "It's just another problem he has on account of his overly sensitive nature: a terrible shyness on awareness of being observed, deriving from his own especially negative opinion of his physical appearance, causing him to blush, stammer, slur and fuck up generally when he only wants to be friendly."

"That's a load of me bollocks!" Co disagreed. "It just gives him an excuse for staying put in his own little world." He continued to bounce.

"You're wrong," I said, "and anyway, he's probably in shock now, or concussed or something, along with everything else. He's not fit to go anywhere. He might even," I said, "have a piece of shrapnel stuck in his throat."

"Bollocks!" Co said again, and then left off Anto, to take hold of his forearms, pull him upwards and abandon him to sway dicily, until he stumbled forwards and landed his head in my lap.

"There!" I said, feeling vindicated.

But Co only laughed: "Well now," he said, "I can see now why you're standin' up for him."

Embarrassed, I couldn't but knee Anto's head away.

"Ox noc yo toh!" he said

"There!", I said again, "we'll just have to leave him behind and go on as before." But Co kept smoking his cigarette: "I didn't know I had it. I swear! ... Did ye want a drag?"

Handing it back to him, he pulled hard, before pressing the smouldering tip into Anto's face, and saying: "Arise hunchback and walk."

And before Anto's cheek was near properly roasted, he did, and none too shakily either.

"There!" said Co.

We followed on, the argument unresolved.

* * *

More bombs and my past life rolled out before me – Herbert had arrived just in the nick of time! But then that was a speciality of his, which led me to to think of other occasions when he'd done the same, and, initially, about Patrick's party.

Patrick had had a party once, for what excuse I can't remember, it certainly wouldn't have been for his birthday: out of respect for the memory of their departed mother, Jimmy's father had prohibited those acknowledgements, not even deferring to his worship of Patrick's true, biological father who, to Patrick back then, was still no more than "The King."

But he, Patrick, hadn't seemed that pleased when we, Roly and myself – it was way back then – arrived. I had assumed that Jimmy had invited us because Patrick had no friends of his own, and that he would have been delighted to see us. But he barely nodded at us when we entered, and went straight back out to his dishes.

Sitting down, I whispered to Jimmy, not that I was afraid that Patrick would hear; he was too busy banging things about in the kitchen, but that Jimmy's father on the couch might, and that he'd wake up to sing at us in Scottish, and send us out for more cigarettes and ice-cream. "He doesn't seem to happy to see us," I said, "I thought he would have been, havin' no friends of his own?"

But Jimmy surprised me: "Yes he has," he said, "loads of them, and even more now since he joined the band. They should be here any minute!"

"Patrick's in a band?" I was totally impressed! I'd never imagined him as the type.

"Well not a real one," Jimmy admitted, "just one of those with trumpets and horns, and all that kind of oul nonsense."

"What does he play?" I asked.

"Well nothin' really yet," Jimmy was honest, "but they let him hang around and make the tea. And," he said, "he's savin' up to buy a clarinet."

"They're goin' to be very big," he added, after a pause.

So we waited excitedly for these budding stars to arrive, only to be rewarded with the prevailing ones: Mickey and two of his mates roared in - the Conroys were surely a tight-knit family! And after waking Jimmy's father to get drunk again with, they sat on the floor smoking and eating Patrick's freshly-made delicacies.

Although, personally, I thought that the party was a great

success, even if the band never showed; who'd want to listen to that kind of stuff, anyway! And we were all enjoying the goodies. But Patrick didn't look happy at all, and wouldn't speak to anyone, except to ask us if we had enough of everything, and was their anything else that we "desired"; he could be very sarcastic, by times, and it was there that the trouble was starting.

When he appeared in the apron and rubber gloves that Anna had bought for him, his only present (Now there was a friend, but she wouldn't have been allowed to be there – by either side!), and asked that same question, one of Mickey's friends sniggered loudly into his rice-crispy cake, and again then when Patrick returned, refusing to look at him, but giggling at his own reflection in Mickey's shiny boots of leather.

And Mickey wasn't taking it well, that was plain for all to see: the colour had drained from his face, and he just kept staring at the wall across from him. The other one, though, I have to say, was behaving himself very well. Not getting involved, he continued to study the same page of the 'Jackie' magazine, that Patrick must have also gotten from Anna, only lifting his eyes, every now and again, to pass on the, extra-long, hand-rolled cigarettes that they'd been sharing.

But Jimmy's father was coming to again, and Jimmy was getting very edgy beside him, and Mickey's mate carried on tittering, and I was sure that the place was about to erupt – I was wrong!

There came a loud knocking on the front door. Answering it; it seemed that everyone else had either buried their heads in their hands or run to hide behind the sofa, Herbert stood there holding, along with his brown paper bag (Now that I come to think of it!), a long cardboard box. He brought it inside, laid it on the floor and removed the lid, to rise and present Patrick with (He left again straightaway, of course!) ... guess what?

No, I was wrong again: It wasn't a clarinet! It was, apparently, a thin whistle, but a large wooden one that Herbert had crafted himself in Uncle Jimmy's yard, and Patrick was so delighted that he retired immediately to his room to to play on it. An air of jollity befell all.

Afterwards, I told Anna the story and she called it "The Magic Flute."

* * *

Agnes came running in one day all excited, dribbling the chocolate from her mouth that she'd stolen from the "High Infants" – I'd seen her!

"Ma, Ma," she said, "there's an oul fella in the laneway and he's after showin' me his thing. It was horrible Ma," she cried, "it was all purple it was, and he was shakin' it at me, and it had this little eye and ..."

Kate ran screaming too, but not before she'd warned us to stay put, so that by the time we did reach the scene of the alleged crime an angry mob had already gathered; Kate knowing who to scream to, and Agnes not having been too upset to alert the right few on the way home. The angry mob had a problem though: the subject of their anger was already comatose, decked out by his own hand and the bottle of 'Marie Celeste' that lay beside him.

From the back row, I gazed respectfully at the tramp: I call him that only because that's how he would have been known at that time, wearing as he was the dirty brown coat supplied by 'Tramp & Wino Outfitters Ltd.' who, somewhere, most have mysteriously existed, and the heavy hair that was perfect for being gungy and matted. I had it myself; people often commented on it when they visited, and, I supposed, couldn't think of anything else positive to say about me. Another possible career choice? I was already doubting if I would really make it as a cowboy or a rock-star.

Anyway, the crowd stood around discussing his fate, while he, outside of it all, lay there caring not a jot about any of them. The women were beginning to snipe at each other, and then at their respective men, particularly, while the men, with their rolled-up sleeves, probably regretting that they hadn't worn their own overcoats; the lashing rain returning, smoked cigarettes and began to speak of football, when Agnes shamed them into action: "What's wrong with you all?" she piped up, "Why don't you do something? Are you all afraid of that lousy bastard? Ah sure," she sneered, "why don't you just let him away with it, and he can tell his friends and they can all hang around here wavin' their yokes at people." (She could be as sarcastic as Patrick!)

Conscious then that she'd blown her cover, that it would have been noted that she wasn't too traumatised to return to the arena of her violation, she took to a hysterical sobbing – she was brilliant at it! She shook and she rattled, she gasped and she rolled, she choked for breath, the tears trailed down her filthy face.

It was more than the crowd could take, and then, of course, there was the honour of the neighbourhood to be conserved, verging as it was on becoming a haven for flashing wastrels and other wandering deviants. The shirt-sleeved men, so inspired, lifted their culprit and slapped his face in a manner that could have been construed as, either, an over-vigorous attempt to bring him around, or, a clinically exacted method of smashing his jowls. They walked a thin line, but were saved from it by Herbert's intervention.

Suddenly, appearing from nowhere (Wherever that is?), he approached the shirt-sleeved men, and gesturing first toward the wall, then the tramp and finally Agnes, he said: "Is it not the walls bounding narrow experience that maketh a man your enemy?" Now, from where I was standing, I wasn't able to grasp the exact wording, but it was definitely around there! And it worked: the shirt-sleeved men responded. They unhanded the tramp, dropping him back to where they'd found him, he probably just putting it down to another disturbed dream, so that not even Agnes could stop the crowd dispersing.

POSTSCRIPT: I hadn't noticed Jimmy's presence there, but he informed me afterwards that it had been, and, more so, that from it's hidden vantage point, he had caught every word that was spoken. Herbert, he told me, had actually warned the shirt-sleeved men that: "Agnes or not," if they didn't release the tramp, he'd put their heads through whatever part of the wall they felt best suited them. A sincere, if mistaken, version: Jimmy had obviously just misinterpreted the "wall" thing.

And then there was the other alternative, the popular one, which would have been hilarious if it hadn't been so wrong, although it was based soundly on Agne's own reputation for perverted character: That Herbert had simply pointed out that Agnes had been caught spying by the tramp while he was having a quiet piddle against the wall, so that she, enraged, ran screaming. Her denial though, for once, put her and I in accord.

As Herbert would have said: "The majority are always wrong."

* * *

The men were becoming restless; they were unable to find the highway. They imagined that they felt like people did when they are lost in a desert and panic begins to slip in. The hunchback, scouting the terrain to the front, was taking the rap for it.

"Where the fuck are ye bringin' us hunchback?" Co demanded, kicking him on again.

Those people in the desert, though, must have had at least the occasional mirage to lift them, and I doubted if they would have exchanged their broiling sun for our twilit shellfire, even if we had grown quickly immune to it; only dropping to the ground now when the shockwaves sent us there. Well speaking for Co and myself, that is: Anto took a rest at every opportunity. And, fortunately, we were able to hold on to no more than our earlier injuries; my own cuts and bruises maybe not amounting to much here, but in another world I would have been proud to display them.

As I was the only one with two sound legs, and was forced to amble and slow, and halt and catch up again, in order to keep the line, and being probably the most restless, I'd even volunteered to replace Anto at the head of it, not that Co would sanction it: "Ye will in yer bollocks!" so that I had plenty of opportunity to examine the typical war-time carnage: Headless men communed with heartless women; bomb-scarred farm vehicles blocked the path for herds of abandoned cows; burnt out dogs had donned sheepskin coats; the queer knelt and kissed the feet of a priest (I'd heard that one before?); a putrid pond played host to stagnant frogs; the goose laid the golden egg ...

"I always hated the fuckin' country," Co observed.

Then sighting some trees, and, I suppose, in the absence of any hills, we headed for them. But once there, we didn't know what to do then. Co kicked them, but there weren't as useless as he'd said they were, because we saw two people approaching, who didn't seem to be able to see us! Co quickly voiced his recognition: "It's Bo!" he said, "It's Bo with a mot!"

He made to run towards them, but I blocked him, pleading caution: "Lets wait," I said, "Let's wait and see what they get up to."

"What are you ... some kinda pervo?" he asked, trying to move away again, "Bo's sound like that...we can all have her!" he said, "That's of course, if we want to?" he added, glaring at me. "Even the hunchback," he said then, "and I'd nearly pay to watch that!"

"They might," I lied, "lead us to the highway!" But Co didn't care.

"Wait!" I tried again, "Why not just use her first, and then we can all screw her afterwards?"

He fell for it! "Okay," he agreed, "but I'm in first!"

The trees, although barren of any foliage, had trunks broad enough to conceal us as the couple passed on by. Mary was just as Joseph had described her.

"What a fuckin' ride!" Co lusted after her, "did yis see them fuckin' trupenny bits! What's she hangin' around with a horrible cunt like Bo for?"

I took his point, even if I was always going to be much more likely beguiled by her radiantly beautiful, high-cheeked-boned face; her eyes that spoke of supreme kindness, and probably ultimate wisdom too; her lips that sparkled divine; her hair shining dark as a starlit night; her sleek, peeky- out tongue; her pert little ..."

"What a fuckin' ride!" Co said again.

"C'mon, put it away," I said to him, and revealing nothing of the goddess's identity, we set off in pursuit.

* * *

The openness of the ground, combining with the bad light restricting us to following so closely, wouldn't have made our detection difficult, but the couple, enchanted as they'd appeared to be, strolling along hand-in-hand, found no reason to look behind them, their careless progress being easily matched by even the worst of us. But then Co would never be satisfied: "What the fuck is he up to," he wondered of his old mate, "why isn't he knockin' the arse of her by now?"

I glanced back at him, and was surprised at my guess at his age. Put some hair on the baby-bald head, just a little bit on the top and around the temples, and you could, quite easily, place him in a darkened suit inside a pub or a bookies shop on a Saturday afternoon. If you really wanted to, you could send him home later to snore and fart for his wife and about three kids. You could put him in a ten-year-old car with fur on the seats and around the steering wheel too, with speakers and big brake lights on. Maybe then, you'd stick a ladder on the roof and send him off to work with his flask of tea, and his bread-wrapper packed sandwiches. You could have him say: "How's it goin'?" to Mick and Joe, as well as to John.

You could buy him a pair of cheap runners to go with the suit. You could fatten his legs and shorten the trousers so that they cleared his foul-patterned socks, forever reminding him of gone-by days. You could take off the hair again. You could give him bowel problems and heart attacks. You could rid him of the teeth. You could make him cough and wheeze and leak. You could lay him out and mark him up as "Co who?" I looked ahead respecting that old "fuckin" face, "fuckin" everything, as it still was too.

"I've a pain in me bollocks," he was saying now, "I'm starvin', I'm freezin' and me fuckin' leg is fuckin' killin' me, and it looks like I'm goin' to get fuckin' pissed on now as well."

True, it had got cooler, and from above us, in spurts, the sky was ejaculating a sopping blackness.

"Fuck this for a game of cowboys," he went on, "I'm goin' to go up to yer woman and find out where I can get some fuckin' nosh and a warm place to kip. And then," he said, "I'm goin' to ride the fuckin' hole of her, and Bo and the rest of youse cunts can all go and shite!"

"No wait!" I said, "Let's wait a while and see what transpires. Let's not interfere, but allow things to evolve into what they would become. Lets not partake or precipitate. Let's stay outside of it all!"

"Bollocks!" Co said, stumbling, having again lost sight of the ground he travelled on. But I had an unexpected ally: "The darkest hour is before the dawn," Anto announced, and that was exactly how it happened. "To' ye ss su," he said, as we stepped into the newborn day.

Beneath a benevolent sun, we treaded upon a lush green underworld, musically accompanied by the birds whistling from the boughs above us. Anto held to watch them – they shat in his eye! Co laughed gleefully, until they got him too, and then hurled large stones at the branches.

We continued up that garden path until, reaching the picturesque cottage at the head of it, Mary, finding a door in the ivy-covered walls, turned to us, and called: "Come along in boys."

We all looked around, and at each other, in that kind of "Are ye talkin' to me?" mode, before we took the silly, incredulous smiles of our faces, removed our index fingers from our chests, and followed her inside to a large table, whereupon lay what must have been the most delectable spread ever to delight any of our eyes, where she sat then with us, so that we could examine her while we devoured it.

I could never admit it, but it might have been my prayers that our common relationship to Herbert wouldn't bar my way, that Bo intercepted, along with Co's sordid ones, because it was only her soft palms that saved our heads from the table top.

"Now boys," she said, "there's never any need for jealously," and, by way of reassurance(?), upped and led Bo from the room. So, Co and I resheathed our weapons to partake of more salt and vinegar crisps and Jaffa cakes. Anto not speaking of what he knew.

But when the happy couple returned it was only to dissolve the queue, for along with them came a certain masked protector.

"Billy Sikes," Joseph proclaimed, "we have another role for you!"

* * *

Leaving Co and Anto to their own devices, the rest of us went outside and mounted Mary's jeep. Joseph filling the driver's seat had, in respect to his Honda C50, perhaps, over the balaclava donned a motorcycle helmet. I sat beside him, whereas Bo, still grinning imbecilically, clattered in alongside Mary behind us.

Joseph drove us quietly, reflecting on his awful life with Marian, I would have thought, back into the darkness. But interrupting his mood, I enquired, stupidly, where we were off to: I had already forgotten my history; surely it was to Mary's "Hill of Redemption!" But he ignored me, preoccupied as he was with righting a jeep offset by a pile of lying bodies.

"Fuckin' Hippies!" Bo commented from the back, as Joseph, ramming the accelerator hard, freed us from the gunge. Lights blazed ahead of us!

"Relax!" he said, unnecessarily to Bo, at least, "I'll take care of this."

He slowed, allowing us to monitor their approach: The armoured car was on seen nightly on television, the white-suited soldiers surrounding it recognisable, from my own readings, as second world war ski-troops, seemingly unbothered by the absence of snow.

"Halt!" They ordered in German. "Who goes there?" when we were spitting distance of them (Bo, to prove the point, opened his window and stained one of the white-suits with a hard-hawked "gallier."). But Joseph surprised me again by hitting the throttle once more, to send at least a couple of the machine-toting gunners skiting sideways. With bullets exploding about us, I found a floor again, and only lifted myself from it when Joseph had careered us clear.

"What the fuck did you do that for?" I asked, whilst checking for more head injuries, and, "Who were they anyway?" when he didn't answer.

"Who knows?" he replied, "They were dressed as the white army which, though, just have might have meant that they were the black army in disguise, or that they were the white army pretending to be the black army in disguise. Then again," he said, "they could have even been the white army as themselves. How can you ever tell! Anyway, what does it matter ... It was either us or them!"

So Joseph, now the Masked Crusader, brought us safely through that hazardous land, until the road rose with us and the heavy jeep's working harder became the predominant sound. Stopped at a red traffic light (?) I queried this, mainly to break the embarrassed silence. "The bombers," he explained, "rarely bother with the higher ground."

Upwards and onwards, and then more lights, but these emanating from a distant campfire. Two riders approaching, I arrested a slide down my seat again when they arrived friendly. Greeting all, they turned off their engines, as Joseph did the same, to engage us in a polite conversation around the prevailing weather. Agreeing that it was quite cold on the hill alright, but foreseeing little possibility of snow, Joseph motioned me outside and on to the nearest pillion, to wave fondly farewell at the Jeep proceeding us on our own shorter journey; we set down amongst the campfire congregation.

There were about another eight or ten of them, dressed in the same generally bearded and heavily braided way as my escorts. I knew the type, we having some around our own neighbourhood: thirty years of age and older, riding ancient motorbikes, decked out with chains and crosses, wearing decrepit jeans, with brand names emblazoned across the backs of their filthy jackets, heading off to 'God Knows Where,' but only at weekends; the rest of the time they went to work and lived in houses.

So I sat with these "Hell's Angels" and warmed my hands at their campfire, ruminating on the crosses that I myself bore on the backs of them.

* * *

I bit the glass. A long time before, I'd bitten the glass. We were all sitting in front of one of those television programmes about the price of prime heifers, or whatever, that you had no other choice but to have on in those days. The priest that visited Kate had just gone, and having absolved her of all sin, I assumed, had left her in good enough humour to break out the diluted orange. I couldn't explain why I did it, and I still can't, other than that it was summertime, and it was still very bright outside and I was very restless, having nothing else to do.

Nobody noticed right away: Kate was zonked on the couch, and Anna wasn't with us either, absorbed, as she seemed to be, with thoughts really complicated, and Agnes, who gotten herself from somewhere a glass with a stem on it, holding it in her chubby little hand, was busy pretending to be who she wasn't.

I didn't feel it that sore, not at first, even if people boasted about feats like that in those times, my mouth just felt very warm when I chewed the piece that I'd bitten off. I'd taken the rest of the broken glass then, having finished my "Miwadi," and inscribed a cross on the back of each hand, although, I'll admit, they were a bit messy.

It was only when Agnes went upstairs to relieve herself and found the blood on the door, and around the toilet bowl where I'd been sitting, that the alarm was raised. Seeking me out, she gave me a few wallops and then ran downstairs to tell Kate. But it was only at the hospital, when they were putting the stitches into my mouth, that I really regretted it. The one's in my hands though, weren't nearly as bad, and I couldn't wait to get the bandages off and see my crosses.

* * *

So there we sat, and if night didn't become day it became a lighter shade of grey, and along with it came Jimmy's dead brother, Mickey Conroy! Arriving at the camp in full leather regalia, he halted his throbbing stead, but only for long enough for me to: "Hop on Kid!" before speeding off again.

"Kid," was about the best I'd ever gotten from him, other than that it was, "Yermate," as in: "Jimmy Yermate's here!" when he answered the door, having given his own mates time to get out the back way; it being dark, and they mistaking me for the law or someone, that did happen once! Mickey rarely answered the door.

But inside, it was generally "Kid," with a wink and a, "How's it goin'?" although, only when he was in his box: when Mickey was "out of his box," be that from drink, drugs or the pressures of life, or whatever, he wouldn't call me anything at all, just look at me very strangely, but Jimmy would always tell me not to mind him then.

Anyway, I was hoping that he was in his box now, and, more so, that he had the lid securely battened down, and with straps attached, as we hurtled down that mountainside. It occurring to me, how incredible it was that he'd survived for as long as he did, and that when he had been taken out, it had not been by accidental forces.

I trusted him not, and he scared me even more, when at speeds of, what must have been, at least one hundred miles an hour, he adjusted to side saddle, or threw a boot over the handlebars. But still, not wanting him thinking badly of me, be he dead or alive, I, rigid, kept my hands firmly nowhere else but on my own knees. Although, when we made it to the flat where he really opened her up, and then pulled a few "Wheelies" I lost that control and was helpless to stop my feet from dangling over his shoulder-blades. But, he didn't complain, or, at least, not until when, on the edge of a town, we braked to a stop.

A ghost town it was too: The creaking sign indicating it's progress had crossed the population all the way down to nought; the wind blew cactussy bits along the dusty street; the saloon doors quivered on their rickety hinges.

We dismounted, and Mickey, reaching into his leathers, withdrew a bundle of leaflets and aiming a portion at me, said: "This is what we've got to do kid!"

But, before I could take possession, he threw the lot, his and mine, into the air, declaring that: "What we've got to do, and what we're going to do, should never be one and the same thing!"

Upwards and outwards, and backwards and downwards, the missives flew, one scoring a direct hit upon my toe, I picked it up, to read: "REPENT ALL YE SINNERS AND DO WHAT WE TELL YOU TO DO, OTHERWISE YOU'LL NEVER HAVE ANY LUCK", so seemed to sayeth: "THE ONE TRUE CHURCH OF MARY."

"I've had enough of that shite!" Mickey said.

"What shite is that exactly?" I asked, shifting uncomfortably, grateful for the breeze (It had been a really scary ride!).

"That Mary shite," he answered, to my relief, "It's all just a sex thing you know!"

"Yeah?" I said.

"She couldn't control her desires," he explained, "so she started a religion around them, and gets rid of everyone she has afterwards so that they can never expose the truth."

"You mean," I said, "The Hill of Redemption?"

"That's right," he said, "a bullet in the head, that's all they get up there. Except for Joseph, of course, but then they all like to have a man to order around."

"But," he said, "at least she's direct. I mean, they all kill us one way or another once they've had their way with us, and it's usually a slow death; you only have to ask my father!"

"But how did you survive?" I asked, just then recalling that he'd actually been a while dead, but wasn't it Von Psychopath who had said that the boundaries were hazy?

But, he answered: "Well she's very vain, and she thinks that any man who doesn't fancy her must be queer or mad, or both, so she sends us away to live together and make religious propaganda.

Although, it's different with the Hell's Angels," he said, "who even she wouldn't touch!"

"And Herbert," I asked, "What about Herbert?" – I'd recognised the Frank Zappa photo over which her message had been superimposed – "Is he not...?"

"Oh Herbert's alright," Mickey said, "Herbert's a nice bloke, a nice, quiet bloke, but that's all. It's just his mother who's making all the fuss."

"And you," I demanded, "are you queer, or mad, or both?"

"Me ... ?" Mickey hesitated, "Oh, I'm just into motorbikes."

So we stalled, while I examined his incredible perspective, before I said: "So what now ... what do we do now?"

"I'll be Butch," he replied, "and you can be Sundance Kid."

* * *

Butch and Sundance rode into town, shivering in the breeze still, they stopped outside the saloon. Butch pushed through the swing doors, they swung back and struck Sundance beneath the chin. Picking himself up, he was happy to believe that nobody had noticed – he was wrong! Inside a ghostly bartender straightened his face, and asked: "What'll it be?"

"All the money," Butch replied, "Just give us all the money!"
But the bartender refused: "Fuck off!"he said, "you must be

joking, go out and earn your own!"and, "That's a fine looking leather jacket you've got on you."

"Never mind my jacket," Butch said, smiling now and flashing his cigarettes, "what have you got for me?"

"All that you'd want from me is in my trousers," said the bartender, lighting the smoke, "but you're not getting it!"

"Whiskey then!" Butch decided. But, "Fuck off"replied the bartender again. "I doubt you're even old enough, whatever about the kid! Come back when you're able to grow a beard."

Butch and Sundance, pretending not to hear the jibes of the other desperadoes who, playing poker in the corners, were chortling into their beers, retreated on to the street, remarking simultaneously that there were "more pubs than churches." But, even as they did so, someone, somewhere, was trying to redress the balance: the place exploded behind them!

"Na Na Nee Na Na," Butch said, when he stood up unhurt, and, "Fuck it the bike!", when he pulled a piece of it's mudguard out from between his teeth.

So strolling along then, they came upon another hostelry, this one promising to: "SATISFY YOUR TASTES IF YOU WILL SATISFY OURS," they entered and ordered some beans. "Any chance of a coffee with these?" Sundance, who'd never had that kind of opportunity before, asked the bearded attendant. But he told him to "Fuck off" too, and handed them a religious leaflet.

Having finished their beans, they were signposted outback, Sundance being the literate one, to where a party of emaciated and nearly naked men pushed a massive boulder up a hill, identified by Butch as "a pile of shite," but who, when almost having reached the summit, lost control, to let it roll all the way back down again.

Overseeing the attempted conquest of this dung-heap, was a foul-looking, leather-clad, whip-cracking hag of a woman who, it has to be said, bore a remarkable resemblance to Sundance's departed cousin, Agnes. But, rather than appearing frustrated by the, it transpired, repeated failures of her charges, she seem to relish them; whipping strips from the hide of a crucial toiler at a critical time, or stretching out a leg to have a cloven hoof (!) deflect the stone at it's optimum moment. Then, with unconcealed glee, she'd flay the bones of another whimpering wretch who'd fallen, unable to face any more of the unequal struggle. Butch declaring that, "this isn't, exactly, my scene," the outlaws took their leave, but only after pleading, unsuccessfully, with those so oppressed to join them.

Outside the conventions of a western town were being further impinged upon; there appearing before them another group of ski-troops, who immediately opened fire. But they were fortunate in that they found themselves standing beside a more traditional type of disused schoolhouse. Even if, climbing through a window, they encountered the ghost of a "schoolmarm" of a totally different era: "What" asked the geriatric nun, from whose wrinked neck hung not the usual cross, but a glistening metallic 'M,' of the type popularly used as presents for age-denying Marys, of my own time, "do you mean by disturbing my class in this fashion?"

Butch, zipping his chest away from the leering glances of the score or so of giggling teenage girls, who, again it has to be said, shared the appearance of Sundance's other cousin, Anna, replied: "We're being pursued by the white soldiers!"

The girls groaning, the nun explained that they preferred the black ones, then led them away along a maze of gleaming corridors, to leave them at a tiny cell. "You'll be safe here!" she assured.

So they sat/lay on the single bed. Butch, who was doing the lying, interesting Sundance in the copy of "Sexual Pleasurement Techniques for the Religious Devotee" that he'd discovered in the locker beside it.

Enthralled, Sundance perused it, until a real girl, or, at least, an Anna-clone, shocked him by entering the room, leaning over it's solitary chair, hitching up her skirt and saying: "C'mon boys, who really wants to know me?" before he hastened out to the corridor after Butch, who was, though again muttering something about only being into motorbikes, about to preserve at least one of the myths about him.

Leaping in to the air, in an eastern style now, perhaps, he kicked the nun, who'd been waiting there, in the face, and then again, when she'd dropped the gun she'd had pointed at them and had fallen. And again and again, leaving her face a bleeding mess. "Never trust the clergy!" he warned.

"Fuckin' faggot!" though, she still managed to shout after him.

The white-suits, who had followed them in to the building, seemed to be only interested now in the Anna-girls who were writhing on the floors beneath them. So that Butch and Sundance might have been able to walk quietly on by, had not an enraged Wilhelm Von Pyschopath arrived dramatically on the scene. Utilising one of the machine-pistols neglected by his compatriots, he obliterated practically everyone in his sight – Anna-girls and there violators(He said!).

And although poor Butch, caught in the crossfire, was dead again, Sundance was glad that he'd gotten to know him.

* * *

Outside, I waited for Von Psychopath, who'd involved himself with a girl who he'd claimed wasn't quite dead yet. But I was enjoying myself too: swaggering up and down with the gun of a fallen soldier hanging from my neck, I even had the customary cigarette dangling from my lips. "If ma could see me now," the words of that other, lesser known, ditty invaded my brain. If anyone could see me now! For the town was dead again, until Joseph arrived in the jeep, glanced in at the killer - The key to his success with woman, Von Psychopath had said – and his carnage, and remarking that, "That must have been no picnic!" nice guy that he was, and formerly unhappy with women, now that I thought about it, brought us off on one.

Seriously! He drove us up a hill that was neither used in the cause of so-called redemption, nor was the preserve of a bunch of homosexuals apostles, nor procrastinating Hell's Angels, and withdrawing from the jeep a blanket and a hamper basket, of the type favoured by Anna's posh kids in her old books, sat us down to enjoy the fare. And that included, along with the bottles of "pop" and the range of wholesome-looking foods, the battle taking place in the valley below us between the varied forces of the black and white armies. Varied, because along with the troops, armoured-cars and helicopters familiar to viewers of the wars in Vietnam and Northern Ireland, both armies, along with their contingents of knights in clumsy armour, representatives of the clergy, giant crows and mobile fortifications, included in their ranks: TV license inspectors, drug barons, mafioso hit-men, priests and brothers, reverend mothers and sisters, gardeners, naturalists and naturists of all shapes and ages, lolly-pop men and lolly-pop women, butchers, bakers and penalty-kick takers, holy men, Nazi SS officers, and flashers and tramps of all persuasions.

I swigged from my bottle and observed the ebb and flow of the fray, finding it impossible to discern any kind of overall pattern: the struggle seeming to be no more than a series of individual clashes, and if an enemy's lines were breached, black would become white, and white became black, and it started all over again. On and on it went, and if the scene held any authenticity, it was ruined by Joseph's belching and Von Psychopath's farting, which would never have happened at Anna's old parties! Becoming bored then with our lofty perch, Joseph decided that we should lower ourselves down, to become involved with things again.

I imagined that we must, at last, be off in pursuit of the Roly/Ronnie gang, not having forgotten my mission, and why else would the Psychopath be riding with us? Especially as Joseph had handed out sunglasses that must have made us look seriously menacing and mysterious, and allowed Von Psychopath, who had the biggest gun, and so the confidence, to lean out of his window and wave it.

But I was wrong! For soon I discovered that the sunglasses were to protect us from the brilliant sun still beaming over Mary's cottage, and to give pause for thought to the black and white dogs who, otherwise, might have snapped at our heels. But, inside, Co's tail wasn't wagging: "It must be true what they say about dwarves and their like," he told us, morosely, "Mary's had the little runt in with her since she got back."

I looked at him sitting there in exactly the same position as when we'd left him, and was sent away on an older train of thought.

* * *

Co had reminded me of God, or, at least, of what Von Psychopath had said earlier about everyone being but a figment of his imagination, his own consciousness the product of some god's cruel joke.

I'd understood exactly what he'd meant, of course, having been through that same terrible stage myself, and Co's sitting there looking as if he hadn't as much as cracked a knuckle since we'd been away, had brought it, if vaguely, back to me.

In my case, it had come about while walking the road to Conroy's: the realisation that everything was the same as it had been on the yesterday; the same woman chattered at the same garden gates; the same small girls blocked my path with the same skipping ropes; the same lads played ball at the very same "squares"; the same arguments wafted out from the same open front-doors; the monophonic music that blared, did so from the same upstairs window.

"How could it be all so predicable?" I asked myself, "Why was everyone behaving exactly as I expected them to?" I could only conclude that, somehow, I was making it all up, and again as Von Psychopath had felt, that I was, indeed, the butt of some incomprehensible god-joke, that my world was a work of fiction, and that the woman came out to chat, the kids came out to play, Jimmy's father took to the couch and Patrick to the kitchen, only at my approach. At home too, Kate and the girls became animated only on the fall of my step, to embroil themselves in another domestic drama, solely, for my naive consumption. At all other times they did not exist; being then just the not-in-use props of an errant creative deity. Or, could I really believe that I, myself, was the god that had made them all up?

These thoughts terrorised me constantly, but only until I took the god out of it and brought forth the implants; having received the signals from a number of television programmes that pretended to be about spies, mainly. Everyone had one, causing them to behave in their, peculiarly, predictable ways. So the girls kept skipping, the woman talking, the drunks roaring and the maids cleaning. There was enough variety in them, although, only just enough, to keep the whole thing going.

There were the fix-it, build-it, thump-it types fitted, although certainly not exclusively (I was very aware of that!), to the male. There were the "I'm going to get pregnant and married rightaway," females one's, that Jimmy's father had, forever, warned me about. There were the, "What I'm going to be when I grow up," and the, "What are you fuckin' lookin at, you skinny, little bastard" childish issues that, nonetheless, carried an, under-used, facility for future modifications and often came laced with certain ambitions, if only of the "I'm going to learn to behave in a way that will make you feel completely worthless and stupid, which will help me to compensate for being in such a lousy job" sort, which were common in policemen, schoolteachers, and probably TV license Inspectors and social welfare workers too. The implants surely made the world go around!

And there were even the misfit ones: The skinheads and the winos had been implanted too, if only with the, "There go I, but for the grace of God," or, the, "No son or daughter of mine ..." strain, and the, 'if I'm not careful to do what I'm supposed to, I might end up ...' device. They kept everyone on their toes.

Nobody escaped! They fitted them in the maternity hospitals and in the chambers of mothers-to-be after midnight. They were administered by health board nurses and other agents in their clinics. They trawled the schools regularly for anyone who may have slipped their nets.

So, of course, I too had been implanted, and not even with one of the more interesting sorts, but with a common type that had me wanting to be good at football, but better able for sums and spellings, instead. Who knew what was to become of me! But Herbert came along and took out my implant. That's what he did: No mere mortal, He had the power to take them away.

They disintegrated when just being exposed to his presence, either that, or, he'd exert a magnetic force and perform an immaculate extraction. Although, there were some that not even he was able to budge: the cheap types fitted to the likes of Agnes, that had no facility for improvement and were made to be unmoved (In those cases, it was necessary to destroy the whole!). But he took out mine, and Kate's and Anna's too. He allowed Patrick and Mickey to be themselves.

Their father's and Jimmy's, he had left alone. The first was defective anyway; corroded by the sea of alcohol that had for so long washed over it. The other, because Jimmy wouldn't have wanted it removed: not for everyone the freedom to choose – there were casualties! Like Kate, who had been too old to be released, and paid for it now in drink and Valium. And Anna, who'd been always fighting against her constraint, where had she gone to without that conflict to stay her?

* * *

Von Psychopath, with no regard for Co's feelings, pushed past him and through the rest of us into the room where Mary and her hunchback were, allegedly, still copulating. We were shocked to hear another burst of gunfire.

Rushing in, I got there before Joseph to be beside him when he lowered his weapon and stood smiling over the bloody body of the naked Mary. Lighting a cigarette, he said: "I've been wanting to do that for ages."

Anto pulled out from beneath her, his own over-sized weapon refusing to shrink.

"Hor soon is nay god," he said.

"What??" I snapped.

"Whores' sons are no good," he said quite clearly.

The audience wept.

* * *

EPILOGUE

Cocky saw it all. Still walking nights when he got the urge. He threw on his boots and his overcoat, and off he went, varying his directions, hoping not to become too easily identified. Tonight, it was over towards the, six-roaded, traffic roundabout known as "The Cross." It was there that he'd witnessed the torment and crucifixion of the man who he'd called his friend; that other lonely traveller, who, when they'd passed, had never been too good to nod "Hello."

Crouched behind a garden hedge, he'd been masturbating slowly, longing for the click-clack of high-heeled feet, when, instead, he'd got the dragging of heavier ones and the gruff voices that came with them. "There's the black bastard!" they'd called, "There's the bollocks who kicked the shit out of Rolo's mot!"

Cocky sneaked a peek at their skinhead faces, hurrying between the cowering traffic, over to where he, standing tall in the centre of the circle's greenness, attempted not to argue or escape, but accepted his fate, not even saying: "No" when they claimed that: "You are that man! You are the one!" with their first butts and kicks. For he knew, that they would have refused to believe him. For he knew, that they knew not what they did. But Cocky did – for Cocky had seen it all!

Cocky had seen another tall, dark man emerge from a van to deal his blows to Anna, then the girlfriend of the fat skinhead

Brophy, but, just like now, because of his own, sick, personal cowardice he hadn't intervened. She'd survived, although mentally impaired, he'd heard, maybe like her cousin Billy, who'd been found guilty, but insane, of trespassing with intent.

So Cocky watched them leaving Herbert to die on the cross, and then, closing his coat, he went home to fuck again the bones of that other girl: Anna's dead sister, Agnes.

* * *